WHY THE
VADA SELLER
REFUSED

Satish Mandora has been a man on the move. He experimented with different ideas and ventures before discovering his true calling as a success coach. He has made a significant impact to the life of more than 40,000 people globally who have either heard his inspirational talks or attended his life-enhancing training programmes. 'Celebrate Life' are the two words that define his life philosophy of life.

www.satishmandora.com
support@satishmandora.com

WHY THE
VADA SELLER
REFUSED
A SALE

and other simple stories for achieving
the best in life, work and relationships

Satish Mandora

RUPA

Published by
Rupa Publications India Pvt. Ltd 2015
7/16, Ansari Road, Daryaganj
New Delhi 110002

Sales Centres:

Allahabad Bengaluru Chennai
Hyderabad Jaipur Kathmandu
Kolkata Mumbai

ISBN: 978-81-291-3661-9

First impression 2015

10 9 8 7 6 5 4 3 2 1

The moral right of the author has been asserted.

Printed at Repro Knowledgecast Limited, Thane

Contents

Preface

In my journey as a 'success coach', the greatest insights into life have come to me from the simplest of things. They have come from the ringing of the morning alarm, the call of a 'vada' vendor at the railway station, a climb up a hill, my son's endless curiosity about the world and my daughter's uninhibited laughter and zest for life. Wisdom lies not so much in the grand but in the everyday.

Nature, above all, has great lessons to teach us, even through the rhythm of our daily life. A tree in autumn, stripped of all its leaves, is a reminder of the impermanence of things. But if we are patient, we learn another, more important, lesson—that in every ending there is a new beginning, Autumn will give way to spring, and the tree will be full of new leaves again. Change and regeneration are the only constants in life.

Or take an eagle, circling high up in the sky. It teaches us to step back, to rise above the immediate moment and look at the larger picture. It also teaches us the benefits of patience and 'detached attachment': the eagle will follow its prey from high above, and only sweep down when all the conditions are exactly right.

There are a hundred lessons to be learnt from life's natural rhythm. We only need to be open and aware, keep our antennae tuned. And then we need to look a little deeper, listen more carefully, feel more intensely.

The most important things in life are also the most simple.

However, a well-known but, unfortunately, easily forgotten fact of life is that simple things are the most difficult to practise. They are even more difficult to communicate. Which is why this book was as much of a challenge to write as it was a pleasure. This book is about sharing and learning and growing together. It is written in language that we use in our day-to-day living, the language of no-fuss communication. People I met on a train or in the street, books I read and could not forget, old friends I reconnected with after almost a decade, real-life heroes and great minds who touched me—they have all added value to this work. And the greatest teacher of all, of course, has been Mother Nature.

There are no rules for reading this book. You could safely start anywhere and stop anywhere. None of the chapters—though I prefer to call them 'episodes'—is more than a page or two long, and they are arranged in five sections that correspond to what I believe are the five most crucial aspects of our lives: Awareness, Energy, Initiative (or Action), Communication and Relationships.

Very often, life becomes only an extension of our business—earning a living, making profits, networking, devising strategies—and business becomes mere 'busy-ness', where a lot of talk and hectic activity is mistaken for achievement. If you're running around all the time, you've probably lost direction and are going round in circles. I hope these pages will help you find the pause button in your daily routine and be sensitive to what is happening around you, and realize what is of lasting value.

Do mail me your feedback and advice. The process of evolving and growing is continuous and your contribution will matter greatly.

Come Celebrate Life.

Stop. Listen. Think.

Why Do We Work?

The highest reward for a person's toil is not what he gets for it,
but what he becomes by it.

—JOHN RUSKIN

All happiness depends on courage and work.

—HONORÉ DE BALZAC

I was watching my daughter, Siddhi, take her basic lessons in swimming. As I watched her finally overcome her fear and slice through the water without assistance, squealing in delight, my heart was filled with pure joy. In that moment, nothing else mattered. I felt complete, happy with my life and the world.

I was reminded of that feeling and understood its true significance many days later. It happened when a question that my son, Pruthav, asked got me thinking.

Pruthav, then in class 8, was home for his vacations from his boarding school. We were chatting and I casually asked him of his future plans. What did he aspire to become? In the course of the conversation that followed, he suddenly asked me, 'Papa, why do we work?'

Caught off guard, I said, 'We work to make our living.'

But Pruthav's question stayed with me. It was a simple question, yet profound, as most simple things are. I wasn't satisfied with the answer I had given him. It led to considerable soul-searching. While I thought about my son's innocent question, I also emailed some of my 'successful' friends about it, and discussed it with others over a cup of coffee.

Having gathered all their reactions and my own, I sat down on a Sunday afternoon to list the reasons why we work.

I listed 42 reasons. They fell in four categories: monetary, business/professional, personal and social.

Based on this list, I and my team at Square Circles ran a questionnaire to gauge the relative importance of these reasons. Close to 100 people responded. We found the responses were all skewed heavily towards personal and social reasons. Monetary or business reasons were important, too, but personal and social reasons were much more so.

But look around—how many of us realize this? The sad fact is that in the rut of business and material concerns, we seem to have lost sight of what truly motivates us to work. As Steven Covey often says, 'How many of you on your deathbed would say, "I wish I was in my office"?'

Take some time out and write your own list of reasons for why you work. It has helped me tremendously to create a work–life balance and focus on things that are truly important to me.

I am now not at the mercy of things that don't really matter to me (well, most of the time!).

Thanks, Pruthav. It was a billion-dollar question that you asked.

The Right Questions

I keep six honest serving-men
(They taught me all I knew);
Their names are What and Why and When
And How and Where and Who.

—RUDYARD KIPLING

We have all the right answers. But do we have the right questions?

As a success coach, I prefer calling myself a 'Professional Disturber'. I always tell my participants and clients that I like to disturb people. I may not be able to give them the right answers, but I will certainly help them ask the right questions.

It is the quality of one's questions that decides the road ahead.

Challenging the status quo, working against the proven right, is what creates innovation.

It takes a high level of strength to challenge the status quo, especially when it appears to be working just fine. Jack Welch challenged GE's position when the going was good. If Steve Jobs had not asked the question why there couldn't be a product that uses the best mechanism nature has created—the human hand—the touch revolution would not have happened. If Kerry Packer had not wondered why a cricket match could not happen in one day instead of five, Test matches would have still ruled. What if Dhirubhai Ambani had not asked himself this simple yet audacious question: how can we create the world's largest integrated refinery? There are umpteen examples, really. How can a person see his photograph immediately after the shoot is done? Polaroid! (And now digital cameras.) How can solar energy be utilized? Solar cells! And so on.

Only when you question the good does the best emerge.

Learn to ask questions:

What?

When?

Why ?

Where?

How?

Keep on asking 'Why?' Ask yourself this at least five times before you arrive at any decision.

Observe. Think. And you'll find the right questions.

Shuttling to Improve

Education comes from within;
you get it by struggle and effort and thought.

—NAPOLEON HILL

There is only one corner of the universe you can be
certain of improving, and that's your own self.

—ALDOUS HUXLEY

Playing badminton is one of my most favourite activities. It is a regular part of my morning routine. One morning, at about 6 a.m., my badminton buddies and I started on our warm-up and stretches. On the adjoining court, a new player had just joined the other batch. He started tossing the shuttle and spread his arms. As would be natural for a newcomer, he could not connect with the shuttle well. He couldn't catch it in the centre of the racquet and smack or lob it with any precision. The shuttle would often hit the rim of the racquet and drop close to him or land outside the court. Every time this happened, the new player would look at the racquet (which seemed perfectly fine) and examine the shuttle (which seemed fine, too) and shrug his shoulders.

All of it meant to convey that the problem was with the racquet or the shuttle and not with him. We have all done such things from time to time. We've missed a shot and blamed the light or an ill-fitting shoe or a slippery racquet handle. What I wish to point out here is that we tend to look for external reasons when things go wrong, instead of looking closely at ourselves to understand what we lack or what we did wrong and finding ways to improve.

Now, whenever I miss a shot or the drop-shot goes into the net or I can't quite manage the backhand—which I know well is my weak area—instead of looking at the racquet or frowning at my partner, I say, 'Sorry! My fault!' I do this consciously. It isn't easy at first, but it is worth making the effort. You only improve when you accept that you need to.

Upasana

Nothing can stop the man with the right mental attitude from achieving his goal; nothing on earth can help the man with the wrong mental attitude.

—W.W. ZIEGE

Stuff your eyes with wonder ... live as if you'd drop dead in ten seconds. See the world. It's more fantastic than any dream made or paid for in factories.

—RAY BRADBURY

Swami Sukhbodhanandji made a beautiful comment to explain 'upasana', the Sanskrit word that translates roughly as 'sitting (or being) close to', primarily in the context of the divine. Swamiji said, 'Nikrushta vastu: Utkrushta drushti,' which means, 'If you develop an eye for the superiority of existence, you can look for the divine in everything, even in the most ordinary-looking object.'

What a powerful insight!

And don't we humans fail to see the best in the world around us, and in the people we encounter every day? We hanker for and run desperately after things that don't exist and miss the treasures that surround us.

How often do you stop and listen to the chirping of birds after you get up in the morning (if you get up early in the first place)?

Do you notice the innocence in your daughter's laughter?

Do you feel wonderment when your car does 400 km at a stretch without a single misfire?

Do you feel amazed when you Google for information on an obscure word and find masses of information for you to explore?

Are you astonished and grateful when you dial the number of a loved one when you are on a lonely jungle trek and are connected?

Don't you marvel at how easily you read a great work of literature? Thanks to printing technology, to paper-production facilities, to the book distribution network, to the school that taught you to read, to the friend who emailed to recommend a book or article to you, to that great invention called email, to the pair of glasses that aided your weak eyes...

So much to be amazed at. And we complain that life is boring.

Can we develop the Utkrushta drushti, the 'superior eyesight', that Swamiji talked about?

Can we look at life differently and not indifferently?

Speaking in Silence

Silence makes no mistakes.

—FRENCH PROVERB

Silence is an answer to a wise man.

—EURIPIDES

Silence is a true friend that never betrays.

—ARISTOTLE

My days at the Experiential Lab (E Lab) programme devised by Swami Sukhbodhanandji taught me some great techniques of personal realization.

One ritual that Swami Sukhbodhanandji told us to follow was 'Vaaktapasya'. According to Manu, the creator of *Manusmruti*, the discipline of the tongue is the most difficult one. Vaaktapasya is about exactly this discipline. It is about silence.

There was a great temptation to talk, but I resisted it. Initially, my logical brain laughed at the exercise, but as it understood the fading of chatter, I felt a different power.

A new view of things opened up. The trees looked different. I could feel the texture of the bark, the rings in the wood, the subtle shades of green in the leaves, the sunlight filtering through them. It was a good beginning.

After some time, as I connected with the Self, the routine chatter and muddle of life fell away. I was not tense about the functioning of my office, my clients' calls for the quotation that was pending, the training feedback discussions, the pending accounts, the follow up from my publisher, the pending TDS certificates...

I could listen to the melody of the wind passing through the tree leaves.

Even a crow's cawing sounded like a song. (This was probably the reason why my nine-year-old daughter had written in her exam that the crow is a singing bird. Of course the examiner marked her wrong. We, too, told her that she was wrong. But she was right. We grown-ups were the ignorant ones, we were deaf to the true music of the world we inhabit but do not understand.)

As the silence embraces us, we connect with our inner self and with the 'real' world. We can then truly experience our feelings, we can listen to our own talk. This is the first and most important step towards becoming intelligent—emotionally intelligent.

Reflection

Muddy water, let stand, will clear.

—CHINESE PROVERB

Study without reflection is a waste of time;
reflection without study is dangerous.

—CONFUCIUS

Jiten Shende, who was the CEO of G.G. Dandekar Machine Works, shared something interesting with me. He told me, 'I've asked my sales staff to stop going to the shop floor where they waste their time. I've told them that when they don't have much work to do, they should sit and watch the tree outside the window.'

A simple statement with a profound thought behind it. The CEO wanted his staff to Reflect.

People in this seemingly busy world hardly connect with their own selves. These days, when you are interrupted every three minutes via an sms alert, an email pop-up, a telephone call on the landline or mobile, a visitor calling on you, when do you find time to think?

To act big, one has to think big and to think big, one has to sit back and simply Think!

This basic habit of thinking must be included in our daily

routine. And, more importantly, in the schedules of our staff as well.

I would like to share a ritual undertaken by a leading newspaper, *Lokmat*. When Mr Vijay Baviskar, a very able and genuine person in the field of journalism, was the general manager of the Jalgaon business unit, he had instructed his administrative staff to observe complete silence for a minimum of 35 minutes after they began their day in the office. So much so that the operator would not transfer any telephone calls to them during this period. The results were startling. Efficiency improved dramatically, as the staff were able to focus on what they really needed to do, rather than reacting to things that kept cropping up. There were no distractions, so they could identify and concentrate on the important, rather than the urgent.

'Moun', or the ritual of observing silence, has been of great importance in Indian culture. It helps you consider and understand what went wrong during your day. What can be done to better the situation? Can you refer back to the old ideas or client prospects? What is more important to you in your life? What is disrupting your work–life balance? Is your business heading in the right direction? What resource crunch can you foresee two to three years down the line? How are your relationships working out? Are they stagnant? Is there new life in them? How is your child going to take the family mantle ahead? How are his or her friends? Are they worth the time he or she spends with them? Are you giving your children enough time? What habits of theirs do you need to work on?

And then:

When was the last time you practically applied a theory that you read?

Do you really read enough to generate newer and better thoughts?

Are you becoming stereotypical?

What are your unhealthy paradigms and dogmas...?

Looking inwards and developing a patient outlook is the key to personal empowerment.

When will you start?

The Silent Observers

It is the man who does not want to express
an opinion whose opinion I want.

—ABRAHAM LINCOLN

For the past few years our team's corporate exposure in terms of assisting the learning and development initiatives of various organizations has been enriching and insightful, both for us as well as our clients. I recently completed a two-day programme on Emotional Intelligence for the senior executives of Endurance Technologies Ltd. It is a big automobile ancillaries manufacturer supplying to practically every name in the automobile industry, including Honda, Toyota, Bajaj, Hero and Volkswagen.

The programme is a very intimate experience and to get people involved—both with the head and the heart—is very important. Typically, we've seen that the first day, being conceptual by its very nature, seems to be a little dizzying, even demanding. Fortunately for me, people are able to connect even though they feel a little exhausted as the day's session invariably extends by a couple of hours. The programme at Endurance Technologies was no exception. On both days we worked for an extra two hours as the discussions got more meaningful and intimate. But all the 21 participants were fully involved and interactive.

At the end of the programme, as I was packing up my training material and laptop, the banquet waiter walked up and stood beside me, waiting till I had finished. He had been in the conference room, assisting us with our small needs through the day, making our coffee and lunch breaks comfortable. I was unaware of his presence and was speaking to a few participants as I packed my things.

After I was done, the waiter smiled at me. I thought he was expecting a tip. With a plastic smile I reached for my wallet and pulled out a 100-rupee note. The waiter immediately stopped me and said, 'No, no, sir! I just wanted to tell you something. Your programme seems to have been a great success. People have liked it!'

I looked at him, surprised and a little flattered, and yet a little sceptical. 'How do you know?' I said. 'Did you understand the contents?'

He laughed. '*Arre nahin*, sahib. I'm an illiterate man. I won't understand what you say, but I noticed that on both days, no one was dozing in the post-lunch session. They were all alert and actively contributing to the discussion. I've seen so many such programmes where people go off to sleep after lunch. In this one, despite a delicious lunch, people were awake and active.'

I was amazed by how observant he had been, and I was humbled. I made a mental note to always take a feedback from such silent observers. People like him—the astute observers watching everything silently from the sidelines—would give an honest and unbiased feedback.

I felt happy. A so-called unlettered person, a man with superior insight and intuition, had given me a certificate of excellence! I realized then that in life there are so many people we may not even notice, leave alone acknowledge, who are observing and judging us. Normally we are interested only in the opinion of people who matter to us, whether in a personal or professional sense. But often it is people who matter little to us who can open our eyes to important truths.

Always try to pick up signals from these silent observers around you. You'll be surprised how many of them there are.

Nandu's Gift: Slow Management

*Slow down and enjoy life. It's not only the scenery you miss by going too fast—
you also miss the sense of where you are going and why.*

—EDDIE CANTOR

My friend, Nandu Adwani, gave me a great gift on my birthday last year. We'd organized a small party that evening, and in the middle of the party my mobile phone rang. I was about to take the call when Nandu said, 'Satish, give yourself a gift today, don't take that call. And as a rule, stop answering your phone when you're enjoying your meal. Can you do this?' His eyes spoke more than his words. His concern, as much as his comment, made me stop, think and decide. I let the phone ring. If it was important, whoever had made that call would do so again.

From that day onwards, I started practising this kind of deliberate slowing down. I've realized that this gives you not only the pleasure of enjoying your meals in peace, but also the power to say no—to things that interfere with your privacy, things that can wait.

Your personal time has to be totally personal. Technology can now locate you even in your bath, or in the middle of a jungle. It is important to always remember what Marilyn Ferguson has said: 'Before we choose our tools and technology, we must choose our dreams and values. Some technologies serve them, while others make them unobtainable.'

While on a vacation I do not receive calls. I allot fixed times for checking mails. When on a walk or a drive with my family, I 'forget' my phone at home.

After all, the mobile phone is for my convenience, it must be convenient for me to use it.

Thanks, Nandu. That was a true friend's gift you gave me—the power to practise Slow Management.

The Weekly Holiday

*Vacation is that time when you wish you had
something to do while doing nothing.*

—FRANK TYGER

I find it very strange when even on an official holiday, factory-owners and shop-keepers spend at least the morning hours sitting in their work places. What is more intriguing is the reason they cite: *'Ghar mein bhaith ke kya karenge, isliye office chale jate hain...'* (What will we do sitting at home? That's why we go to the office.)

This is particularly true in small places.

I can't understand this. Have people become so addicted to their routines that by default they end up at work even on a holiday? Is there really nothing 'worthwhile' to do on a vacation?

When did they last glance through their children's books? (Do they know what grades their children are in? Or how well or badly they did in their last exams?)

When did they last help their children prepare for an elocution contest or a debate?

When did they last walk by a lake or on the grass in their neighbourhood park?

When did a husband last go out for lunch with his wife? (Dinner is easier. But lunch? Just to break the routine?)

When did they last pick up their favourite book? Or watch the DVD of a classic instead of a loud and tired TV soap?

When did they last spend some time for a social cause?

When did they last buy vegetables or groceries for the family? (This would be a sure eye-opener for a lot of people. They'd learn a thing or two about managing the family budget.)

When did they last find some time to get a good massage or a facial? Or give their child a massage? Or play a board game with the family? Or give their dog a bath?

The fact is, if you are really creative you would never make the mistake of saying, '*Yaar, ye chhutti ke din kya karein, samjh nahin aataa.*' (I have no idea what to do on a holiday.)

I really long for holidays. They rejuvenate me and reconnect me with myself and to the things that matter the most to me.

Talk the Walk

Many people are liberal in principle, reluctant in practice.

—JOHN BURGESS

It is easy to have principles when you are rich.
The important thing is to have principles when you are poor.

—RAY KROC

A couple of days back, after I had returned from yet another hectic schedule of my training programmes, I had a chat with my mother. I don't remember what exactly we were talking about, but I remember distinctly something she said during our conversation. She repeated what she had heard somewhere a long time ago: 'It is easier to merely say things on a public platform than to actually translate your ideas into action in the real world.' As my training programmes and seminars received a good response, the words of praise had probably reached her, too. Of course she was delighted, but she was also worried about my credibility in the eyes of the very people who attended my programmes.

I mulled over my mother's words for a couple of days, subconsciously.

'It is easier to merely say things on a public platform than to actually translate your ideas into action in the real world.'

Two issues come to my mind for people who think this way.

One, even if it is not easy to practise the thoughts one advocates (to the extent that the speaker or trainer himself cannot always follow the routines he recommends) does it mean that the thoughts themselves are not valuable or important? Or is it just a way for people to feel comfortable—that because the speaker doesn't practise what he preaches, they, too, can continue to be the way they were.

Does the human mind think, 'I'm happy because someone else has been corrupted as much as I have been…it means that I'm not alone, so I need not worry. There are many who give or take bribes, so it is okay for me to do it as well'? Or, 'Many people live an ordinary life, so it is okay for me as well. Many have been hit by tough economic times, so it is okay for me to fail'?

No. I would say that what they need to think is this: 'Am I using this as a crutch to make my own limping acceptable to myself? Why am I not taking a stand? Why should I accept mediocrity and failure in my life and business just because some others do in theirs?'

Or this: 'Why should I not gather courage to fight my fears, break my habits and walk on the path of a bountiful living? If I rationalize my lack of initiative and ambition by saying that it is okay in theory but real life is different—then it is a shameful way to justify my own self-defeating beliefs!'

Speaking for myself, unless I had conviction in both thought and action, I would not have found speaking in my programmes—or even writing this book—easy. There are times when my inner meter does ask me a question: 'Do you really believe this?' If the answer is not a definite 'Yes', then it becomes extremely difficult for me to speak and yet sound convincing.

To do that is a kind of lie, and I find it difficult to lie.

The old saying 'Practise what you preach' has a clear corollary: Preach what you practise!

ENERGY
Revitalize your Inner World.

Celebrate Life. Always!

May you live every day of your life.

—JONATHAN SWIFT

Here is an email that someone shared with me, and which I believe is the best practical guide to daily happiness, because it is all about living life to the full:

Life's Little Instruction Book

- ▶ Have a firm handshake.
- ▶ Look people in the eye.
- ▶ Sing in the shower.
- ▶ Own a great stereo system.
- ▶ If in a fight, hit first and hit hard.
- ▶ Never give up on anybody. Miracles happen every day.
- ▶ Always accept an outstretched hand.
- ▶ Be brave. Even if you're not, pretend to be. No one can tell the difference.
- ▶ Whistle.
- ▶ Avoid sarcastic remarks.
- ▶ Choose your life's mate carefully—90 per cent of all your happiness or misery depends on it.
- ▶ Make it a habit to do nice things for people who will never

find out.
- Lend only those books you never care to see again.
- Never deprive someone of hope; it might be all that they have.
- When playing games with children, let them win.
- Give people a second chance, but not a third.
- Become the most positive and enthusiastic person you know.
- Loosen up. Relax. Except for rare life-and-death matters, nothing is as important as it first seems.
- Don't allow the phone to interrupt important moments. It's there for *your* convenience, not the caller's.
- Be a good loser.
- Be a good winner.
- When someone hugs you, let them be the first to let go.
- Be modest. A lot was accomplished before you were born.
- Keep it simple.
- Beware of the person who has nothing to lose.
- Don't burn bridges. You'll be surprised how many times you have to cross the same river.
- Live your life so that your epitaph could read, 'No Regrets'.
- Be bold and courageous. When you look back on life, you'll regret the things you didn't do more than the ones you did.
- Never waste an opportunity to tell someone you love them.
- Remember no one makes it alone. Have a grateful heart and be quick to acknowledge those who helped you.
- Take charge of your attitude. Don't let someone else choose it for you.
- Visit friends and relatives when they are in hospital; you need only stay a few minutes.
- Begin each day with some of your favourite music.
- Once in a while, take the scenic route.

- Answer the phone with enthusiasm and energy in your voice.
- Keep a note pad and pencil on your bedside table. Million-dollar ideas sometimes strike at 3 a.m.
- Show respect for everyone who works for a living, regardless of how trivial the job is.
- Send flowers to your loved ones. Think of a reason later.
- Become someone's hero.
- Marry only for love.
- Count your blessings.
- Compliment the meal when you're a guest in someone's home.
- Wave at the children on a school bus.
- Remember that 80 per cent of the success in any job is based on your ability to deal with people.
- Don't expect life to be fair.

The Great High

Enthusiasm spells the difference between mediocrity and accomplishment.

–NORMAN VINCENT PEALE

Enthusiasm is the electricity of life. How do you get it?
You act enthusiastic until you make it a habit.

–GORDON PARKS

I read about an experiment that was conducted in an old age home where all the residents, aged 60 plus, were told to make one change in their routine. They were asked to do everything quicker. They could walk faster, stand up or sit down quickly, carry themselves to the dining table quickly and so on. Independent observers were shown two sets of photographs of these people—one set was taken before the experiment began and the other two months after. Independent observers compared the two sets of photographs and their analysis revealed that people who once stooped had started walking straight, those who used a walking stick could now walk independently, everyone's skin appeared to be healthier (and medical examination showed their blood flow was healthier, too).

What was the one thing that made the biggest difference in the lives of these older people?

By moving faster they had simply invited enthusiasm into their lives.

It's a Great High!

The big difference between the good and the great is, more often than not, enthusiasm.

And it is contagious.

The origin of the word 'Enthusiasm' lies in the wonderful Greek word 'Entheos', meaning 'The God within.' Is it any wonder that it works miracles?

Motivation is not about a noisy display of enthusiasm. Being loud and being enthusiastic are totally different things. One has its roots in aggression while the other is in assertiveness—the preferred state of living.

Enthusiasm is an outward expression of an inner feeling, the feeling of goodness, or rather, Greatness. Mahatma Gandhi, Indira Gandhi, Nelson Mandela, Amitabh Bachchan, Shahrukh Khan, Aamir Khan, Jim Carey, Sachin Tendulkar, Steffi Graff— name any shining star and you can correlate their enthusiasm with the speed with which they do things.

Walking quickly, climbing the staircase faster, or skipping one flight while doing so, general speedy movement of the body... All of these invite and enhance enthusiasm.

And if you can't make it, fake it. It will slowly become a very real habit.

Children can be a great inspiration to imbibe enthusiasm in our psyche. Play with them; play like them, think like them. It will not only help you get back that diminishing innocence, but also boost your well-being with their enthusiasm.

Don't wait; get started now and recharge your energy pockets!

How Do You Get Out of Bed?

Men are nothing until they are excited.

—MICHEL DE MONTAIGNE

I often ask participants in my training programmes, 'How do you get out of bed?'

Eight out of 10 times people say they snooze the alarm or complain, *'Aare yaar, uthna padega! Ye subah kyon hoti hai?'* (I'll have to drag myself out of bed! Why does the day begin?)

And, unknowingly, this sets the tone for the day.

I honestly feel that if you change this first thought, you can have a different day ahead. After all, the beginning matters a lot.

When I get out of bed it's like I've sprung to life, with a big smile on my face, and I feel, 'Wow! It's time to start a lovely new day!' It gives me a completely new perspective on life every day.

As the tone is set right at the start, the enthusiasm colours my entire routine through the day.

You see, even though we 'climb down' from our beds, we actually 'get up'.

The important meaning here is to rise to a new level.

Mahatria Rā of Infinitheism often signs off his writings with the words 'Excited to be Alive!'

What a great way to think!

Another sure way to add a healthy dose of enthusiasm to your life is to exercise. Loads of articles recommend exercise as a feel-good tool, and so do medical journals. Your family doctors give you the same advice. But I don't see even one per cent of the people around me on the playground, or by the lakeside in the woods, or on a hill, or on the badminton or tennis courts.

Which really is a pity, because a mere 30 to 40 minutes of daily exercise can pump up your enthusiasm like nothing else can.

Even though I travel a lot, the first thing I put in my travel bag is my pair of jogging shoes. About 20 to 30 minutes of jogging or a brisk walk, some 'Surya namaskars' (the origin of push-ups), a couple of sets of crunches—this is all it takes, not only to tone the body, but also to add that invaluable source of internal energy—Enthusiasm!

Perhaps this is the secret of what I receive particular appreciation for after my training programmes—that the energy is always positive and its level palpably high.

My Inspirations

The great man is he who does not lose his child's heart.

—MENANS

It's never too late to have a happy childhood.

—TOM ROBBINS

Mitu and I are blessed with a son and daughter who are wonderful creatures. Their energy is amazing and their cult of happiness and laughter, enviable.

There are so many little things that they constantly remind me of.

When they play Tom & Jerry, and crawl on the floor, it reminds me to enjoy the pursuits of life and to fight for them with a positive frame of mind.

They are amazed by any small gifts that my family members give them. They love to receive gifts and are full of curiosity and eager to open them immediately, reminding us to enjoy and delight in all the gifts that the Almighty has bestowed upon us.

They want to participate in all the activities of their school. In one of the social meets of the school my son, as a member of the school band, also did some stage-magic tricks, danced to a song and performed acrobatics in a circus that the children had staged. His mother was busy back-stage dressing him up for his different roles. He performed with huge vigour and joy. Watching him, I was reminded of how important it is, how rewarding—and, finally, how easy it is, with the right attitude—to give my best in each of the roles that I play in my life—a son, a father, a teacher, a husband, a boss, a businessman, a success coach, a Rotary volunteer, a friend, a brother.

I'm yet to be on the excellence track in any of these roles. And I hate being perfect. But the important thing is the commitment and enthusiasm with which I live each role.

There are lessons I have learnt from my children. My daughter wants to be part of the elocution team at school and also to anchor the social meet. She does both with equal enthusiasm and both equally well. She enjoys the challenge of various competitive exams, yet she doesn't deny herself the thrill of watching *Backyard Science*, *Mad Magic* and *Mr Bean*.

My son, too, has always managed a similar balance between the curricular and the extra-curricular. He would never understand why anyone should have to choose to either study or to play; to him, everyone must, and can, do both.

Young people like these teach us to strike a balance in our personal and professional lives. Rather than rationalizing our so-called worldly wisdom, we need to pause and dare to learn from children.

Foodie!

The more you eat, the less flavour,
The less you eat, the more flavour.

—CHINESE PROVERB

To eat is human; to digest divine.

—CHARLES TOWNSEND COPELAND

Attending a four-day Existential Programme with Swami Sukhbodhanandji was a spiritual feast. Among the things that we were told to practise was 'Anna Purneshwari Upasana'. We were told to look at food as the source of God, leading to Bliss or Anand Leheri. With this feeling of godliness we had to take the first bite, close our eyes and chew carefully and very consciously. Initially, I was a little apprehensive, but follow as we must a guru's teachings, I followed these instructions.

Having done what Swamiji had advised us to, I can tell you that the experience of looking upon food as the very source of God was indescribably blissful. It is impossible to describe the feeling, it can only be experienced.

Like everyone alive, I've been eating from the very first moment of life that I can remember, but it was on that day that I felt the difference between eating and savouring.

In fact, merely observing the food on the plate with complete concentration and respect gave a whole new dimension to this heavenly creation.

For the first time I noticed the beautiful colours, patterns and smells.

A tomato is not simply red; there are differing hues of red in it. There is beauty in the pattern of the seeds embedded in the soft, juicy flesh of the tomato.

A carrot slice had a cream-and-yellow centre and a glowing energy that radiated towards the pink exterior.

The sprouts looked fresh and tender, like nature's little works of art—the germinated roots like delicate, feather-light hooks.

The chapatti was puffed and warm, marked with lovely roast marks.

The humble rice and dal had a rich, natural aroma. I could smell the 'tadka' and the spices that had been blended smoothly.

The curd was pure white and I could feel the cool touch on my tongue even before I had tasted it.

As I took my first mouthful, I closed my eyes and chewed slowly, imagining that the food was giving me eternal energy. I hadn't had half as blissful an experience eating any of the several thousand meals I had had in my entire life till then.

I think that somewhere in our daily routine our basics have gone wrong. We gulp our food, often when we're busy on the phone or watching TV or arguing or worrying about a domestic or business matter. All of this creates stress. We don't experience feelings of well-being and love or gratitude while we eat. We should, because the making and eating of food is a magical, enriching experience.

Food may fill our stomach, but the heart and mind are still empty when we eat without awareness, without respect for the food and for ourselves. This source of calorific value not only gives us energy to live but also divine power to thrive.

We must evoke the right feelings when we eat and savour our food. Serenity, compassion and the bliss of being egoless are just a few by-products of this act.

Some Play and Work Makes
Jack a Great Guy!

Every production of genius must be the production of enthusiasm.

—BENJAMIN DISRAELI

I always tell people that in my experience, when you need to hire new staff, you should look for them on a jogging field or in a park, a sports complex or a gymnasium. You'll make a great choice.

(Incidentally, have you noticed the hawkers selling their wares on trains or at traffic signals? Have you noticed how charged up, how full of enthusiasm they are? They need to be, or they won't make a living.)

If you want to do something about the energy in your organization, start a compulsory ritual of 20 to 30 minutes of morning exercise. Put up a small gymnasium, or get a volley ball or a couple of cricket balls and bats. A mere half hour of games and exercise can add tremendous value to the eight hours that these people will put into their work. It not only breaks the monotony, but also enhances team spirit and, more importantly, keeps them young at both body and heart.

My office staff and factory workers have shown a tremendous positivity since they started playing cricket for about 30 minutes every day. Mind you, they haven't asked for time off from the scheduled work hours. They simply finish their lunch early. They are excited to play.

Are you excited to live?

You Create the Atmosphere

All animals, except man, know that the principal business of life is to enjoy it.

—SAMUEL BUTLER

It was a slightly dull start to the day for me. I should have rested after my hectic schedule of the previous week. But without paying heed to the body's demands I went to the badminton court, a little sluggish. The mood in the big hall was equally dull. Only four or five other players were stretching lazily to warm up for the game.

I could sense an energy drain in the atmosphere.

A few minutes later, my badminton pal and a renowned lawyer, Sagar Chitre, entered the hall, singing loudly—'Masakali' from the film *Delhi 6*. Not only was he singing but also enacting the duck walk, enjoying the song and his act with a wide grin on his face. In a few seconds the entire atmosphere changed.

What felt like a dull beginning became a joyful morning. My exercise speed doubled and there was a sense of happiness and good cheer in the hall.

Can you connect with this experience? So often, when a tense person enters the room, a feeling of unease descends upon the entire group.

Someone yells on the telephone at a supplier and the entire office becomes tense.

You enter your home angry and irritated, back from a rough day at work, and the children quickly leave the room. They can sense, even before you have spoken a word, that their dad is in a bad mood.

Can you see that moods are contagious? You create your social ambience.

Daniel Goleman talks about this neural effect at length in his masterpiece *Social Intelligence*. The message he gives us is simple: We are wired to connect.

It is very important for us to be conscious of our moods. We need to make a deliberate effort to create a positive energy in our homes, work places, at social gatherings, even in public places.

Feelings are grossly contagious. We will receive only what we give. Whether we want to be happy or unhappy is entirely our choice.

Hill Se Dil Tak

A challenging trek is good exercise for the mind.

—ANONYMOUS

Early one morning, at about 6 a.m., Tushar Chothani, my co-trainer and a very enthusiastic young man, my nephew Nakul and I set out on a morning walk.

We were in Pusad, a small town in Vidharbha, Maharashtra, conducting a training programme for the students of the Babasaheb Naik College of Engineering. As we walked down the road to the town's outskirts, the air began to feel even fresher than in the college campus, and there was a deep silence—an energetic silence!

As usual, very few people were out at that early hour.

We came to a hill that looked steady, powerful and ancient in the half-light. We decided to climb the hill.

When we were halfway up, we stopped and looked down at the cityscape, yet to stir and begin with the day. Our little halt helped us catch our breaths. Then we began climbing up again. I deliberately took the difficult path up. It was steep and rocky.

It can be fun to challenge yourself physically. It contributes to mental toughness.

With a little effort and lot of balancing I reached the hilltop to be welcomed by Tushar. Nakul joined us after a couple of moments. I knew that something of what we had achieved by challenging ourselves would rub off on the students we were training.

These unusual treks, climbs or jogs give us back the spirit of enterprise and adventure, and the resolve, that we lose in our daily stress and strain. As they enhance our playful enthusiasm, they also add a dash of spice to our physical stamina and our desire and ability to explore the unknown and test our limits.

Coming down the hill was an equally invigorating experience. We bounced and hopped and jumped downhill—the child was very much alive and well within each of us.

Try taking walks in hilly terrain, practise a long jog or a walk in a forest whenever possible. It will give you tremendous satisfaction. It will show you that you are still young at heart —and that matters!

The Joy of Work!

I never work hard when I am working;
I only work hard when I am not working.

—IRVING CAESAR

Nothing is really work unless you would rather be doing something else.

—J.M. BARRIE

Dr Pradip Joshi and Dr Seema Joshi are our family friends. Pradip is a psychiatrist and Seema, a professor of marketing management.

Pradip, now in his late 50s, was a regular badminton player till recently, before he chose a daily morning walk instead. I would see him out on his walk in the mornings when I left for my game of badminton, and I would wave to him. Shortly after I last saw Pradip at the badminton court, Mitu and I met the Joshis on Diwali, and I asked Pradip about his morning walks.

'I've decided not to do anything as a chore or a task,' Pradip told me. 'I'll do it only if it gives me pleasure.'

I thought about what he had said, and it made perfect sense. At his age, he was financially secure. He had taken care of his responsibilities—personal, professional and social. He had no point to make, no obligation to do anything he did not really want to.

This was an important lesson. Very often, we take up a task only because it is the done thing, regardless of how we truly feel about it. We are driven by our obsession with being 'regular'.

Even a game of badminton can be taxing sometimes, more of a habit or a duty than a pleasure. Why not replace it with a jog or a workout, then?

Going to your work place every day—irrespective of your real contribution at work—can become a burdensome ritual. Couldn't you work from your home, in that case, and manage just as well as you would in an office?

Going to a party as a social commitment can get boring. Why not go with your spouse for a moonlight coffee?

Watching a TV soap becomes monotonous business but you keep doing that simply because you and the family have been watching it out of habit for months. Perhaps you could invite the entire family to watch some video, like *The Secret* or *In Pursuit of Happiness* or even *Kung Fu Panda*?

Why read a book just to finish it, whether it adds to your knowledge or not? There's nothing to prove—put that book back in the shelf and pick up another, by a different author, on a different subject.

There's little to be gained by talking about the same things to the same old friends if your heart isn't in it. Couldn't you call up an old college friend with whom you've only been exchanging comments on Facebook?

I am not against routine or habit—they have their place and can be both useful and comforting. The point is, if these become a burden or a nuisance, or if they bore us, we need to spice up our lives and feel the true joy of doing something that we *want* to, rather than something that we *have* to. Otherwise we end up doing a 'job' and that adds no value to our life or the lives of people around us. Needless to say, we also end up adding stress to our life.

Learn to connect with your feelings when you do anything. Make a mental note about your energy level and the mood that you create when you are in the moment of delivering your responses to a daily chore. And then decide if you should change what you do and how you do it.

Thank you, Pradip dada, for the insight.

DO IT
Execution is the Key to Success.

- -

Inaction

I never worry about action, but only about inaction.

—WINSTON CHURCHILL

Elbow grease is the best polish.

—ENGLISH PROVERB

Professor Sumanthra Ghoshal, a great writer and strategist of the London School of Business, had once put forth a very powerful question: 'What was that one thing which you wanted to do, which would have had a significant impact on your business or professional life, but for whatever reason you did not do it?'

In some ways, this is a scary question. For most of us, there would be more than a few things that we wanted to do, or should have done, but didn't.

All of us plan. All of us speak of so many things to do—change, grow, expand. But...

We just maintain a status quo.

We might want to do a great number of things: cultivate the habit of rising early; start on an exercise regimen; make time to read; practise yoga, take your daughter to the counsellor; spend time with your mother; plan a family picnic; check on the dead stock in your factory stores; meet your most important customers; sit across the table with your production team; change the system of MIS (Management Information System); explore a new area for your product; plan the accounting system for next year; meet your family doctor for the annual check-up; check out a few colleges for your son who is still in class 9 but who would need this information after a couple of years; call upon the music teacher because your wife and you want to sing a duet in your social club; attend a few international conferences that would give you an opportunity to collaborate in your business; visit a family friend to celebrate the birth of his grandchild; register for your doctorate...

The list goes on. A thousand and one things that are important to us, but do we do anything about any of them?

Our biggest problem in our personal, social and professional life is INACTION.

Can we simply get 'in action'?

Being Free

My private measure of success is daily. If this were to be the last day of my life, would I be content with it?

—JANE RULE

Do you work to remain free, or is it because you are free that you work? This is a question that you must constantly keep asking yourself. Or else you get into the loop of 'busyness' and end up doing trivial work and hardly find time for the truly important things.

Yesterday, on the train, I was chatting with Sandeep Sikchi, a close friend of mine who is a passionate architect. I told him about this book. Sandeep responded with the information that he, too, had written about 20 pages on 'Detailing in Architecture', but that was two years ago, and he hadn't added anything to the manuscript since. He also said something about a dream he had of owning some farmland some day and working on it.

Why do so many of us dream a dream, work towards it a bit in a rush of enthusiasm, and then simply forget to pursue it? In the daily grind, we rarely remember the dream, but it never quite dies.

It is natural, therefore, that we often can't deliver our best, because most of our time is spent on things that appeal to us less than what our dreams are about. We start avoiding responsibility, procrastinate and 'kill' time and other resources. We fill our work hours with to-do charts with trivial chores and feel that we're working hard.

And then wonder why we don't see any results. We wonder why we're failing, and why it is that others succeed despite being so relaxed in their approach. Then we blame Lady Luck for deserting us and descend into inaction. Everything we do is half-hearted.

This is hardly surprising. Passion is a natural outcome of doing things that we really wish to do. And it is only with a powerhouse of passion that we realize great energy within us and are able to come through tough times, overcoming every possible hurdle in our way.

If you don't work to remain free (in order to pursue your dream) you can work 16 hours a day all your life and achieve nothing of substance.

The Vadawala Karmayogi

Amateurs hope; professionals work.

—GARSON KANIN

God sells us all things at the price of labour.

—LEONARDO DA VINCI

People forget how fast you did a job, but they remember how well you did it.

—HOWARD W. NEWTON

I was travelling back home from Mumbai by the Sevagram Express after a meeting with the energetic director of G.G. Dandekar Machine works Ltd, a Kirloskar Group Company.

At Igatpuri Railway Station the train takes a halt for about 10 minutes. This particular time, on the adjoining platform, another train was ready to leave for Mumbai. The hawkers were busy trying to sell their goods that included chai and vada.

As the signal turned green, the train on the other platform began moving. One of the vadawalas kept moving along with the train, desperate to make a last-second sale. One passenger asked for a plate, which the vadawala promptly gave him with one hand, balancing on the other hand the big tray holding his merchandise. The train had gathered momentum by now but with the finesse of an athlete, the vadawala collected the money, returned the change, and completed his sale.

What appealed to me was the satisfied look of on his face —the look of an experienced professional who had carried out a transaction successfully. But he did not linger on his success. Almost immediately, he was running towards our train where he restarted the process of selling his vadas.

He had unparalleled hope in this process. He was trying to make a sale although this train, too, had started moving. He was fully involved, making his sales, keeping his senses alert, not getting carried away as he kept pace with the train—cautious not to overstep, for the danger of falling down was very real. He exhibited the same caution by refusing one last customer because the speed of the train was by now too fast and he knew he would certainly endanger his life if he tried to make more money. I found this a true expression of his 'detached attachment'.

And then, most importantly, he did not keep rejoicing, or regretting the loss of an extra sale—he immediately turned his focus back to his job. He obviously did this every day, with the same mix of energy and restraint, hope and realism.

Aren't these the traits of a true 'Karmayogi'?

I bought the vadas from him. They reminded me of the prasadam at the temples.

The Polishwala's Rhythm

A man at work at his trade is the equal of the most learned doctor.

—HEBREW PROVERB

My grandfather once told me that there are two kinds of people; those who do the work and those who take the credit. He told me to try to be in the first group; there was much less competition there.

—INDIRA GANDHI

Mumbai is full of rhythm. The traffic jams, the local trains, the dabbawalas, the office-goers, the taxis, the BEST buses; everything and everyone have their own rhythm. This is why people go back to being normal even after the worst calamities, whether man-made or acts of nature. The city gets back on its busy feet—fast, really fast.

In the rush and bustle, we often don't notice some very revealing things about the city's inhabitants. One person who is worth watching is the polishwala or the shoe-polish man sitting on the railway platforms at the local railway stations.

There are many polishwalas at the stations, all sitting in a row. The knocks of their brushes on the wooden 'shop counters'—the wooden stands for their clients to put their feet on—call your attention without fail. You turn, and you choose one and walk over to him.

No one tries to lure you to come to him and not go to the next polishwala. A great lesson in teamwork—no manipulations or one-upmanship, each one has an equally fair chance.

The moment you keep your foot on the chosen man's wooden counter, one of his hands makes sure that the alignment is right so that the brush won't slip beyond the territory of your shoe, go over to the sock or the fabric of the trouser. In the meanwhile, the other hand has already started with the basic clean-up.

Opening the polish tin, he uses a finger to put the polish on your shoe. Nice and wholesome, no stinginess. The cream covers your shoe sufficiently and it seems to enjoy the rich soft nutrition.

The polishwala has, before you know it, quickly changed the brush with the grace of a ballet dancer, one hand supporting and balancing the shoe. His synchronized polishing of the shoe, his rhythm, the swaying of his body, all make him some sort of a 'Sahajyogi', a naturally enlightened being.

A single knock on the wood is an indication to swap your feet. The process repeats itself for the second shoe. The first one is ready and glowing.

Using a special brush to shine, he vigorously massages your shoe, till you feel the tickle inside, on your sock-clad foot. The final touch is a thin strip of nylon cloth being rubbed over and over the shoe for that ultimate shine.

Each shoe is now an artist's masterpiece.

You silently hand over the coins to him, which he drops in the small drawer attached to his shoe-shine box and looks up for the person behind you.

No words are exchanged; it's a perfect mime play that projects his satisfaction at a job well done.

Who else, other than this polishwala, can teach you time and motion study? Fredrick Taylor must have visited Mumbai to understand this theory so popular in production management.

The placement of the polishwala's resources, the brushes (coarse and fine), the polish box, cream box, nylon strip, used toothbrush, his work station, its dimensions, elevation, inclination, the drawer within, the in-soles and laces, everything is so systematic and so organized!

It gives a great lesson for manufacturing set-ups.

And then his personal involvement and his rhythm—that's the unmatched quality for the onlooker. It is what most of us experience when we are truly in the flow of our chosen work.

Leader...Do You Really Need a Title?

Leadership is action, not position.

–DONALD H. McGANNON

It was 23 October 2008—an important day because I met Robin Sharma, one of my favourite author–speakers, face to face. I spent the entire day listening to him, sitting in the front row at his Leadership Seminar.

Robin loves to talk about 'Leadership without title'. He has exemplified leadership in small, seemingly meagre professionals like a carpet fixer or a taxi driver.

It was my turn to experience leading without a title that evening.

My son, a guitar enthusiast, longed for an electric guitar. I wanted to surprise him. My nephew, Nakul, and I went to Furtado, a leading music shop in Mumbai. Although not furnished futuristically, it has a rich vintage look. Sushil, the salesman, helped me select the ESP40 model from the catalogue but, to my dismay, it was not available in the showroom. The records showed that one piece was available at its Mahalaxmi warehouse about an hour away. It was time to close and I thought the shop assistant would probably not be interested in fetching it from the warehouse. I told him that I had a train to catch and that I wanted to surprise my son with the guitar as his birthday gift.

The shop assistant said he would go and fetch the guitar and that I could come back after an hour and a half. Nakul and I had a quick dinner and returned to Furtado at about 7.40 p.m. We were the only customers in the shop and everyone was eager to leave. But they kept on talking to us, showing us keyboards and drums, made me play the Yamaha Drum Station. Someone started playing the keyboard to old Hindi film songs and the mood was of high energy even when the day was to close.

My guitar came at about 8 p.m. The box, extra strings, cover, belt, all were kept ready. Suddenly, it struck me that the guitar was heavy and that my son travelled four times a year between his boarding school and the house. It would need some secure packing. I enquired and in five seconds Sushil was on the ladder to fetch a hard case. Above all, he did not charge me for the case, saying that it was a gift from Furtado!

The staff at the shop had stayed back for almost an hour extra, without even once complaining about the late hour. They were smiling and pleasant throughout, giving more value than the money that I finally paid for the guitar.

And the ecstasy on my son's face when I reached home was priceless.

Thank you, Furtado! You truly have people who lead without a title.

No Crysis!

Problems always appear big when incompetent men are working on them.

—WILLIAM FEATHER

Many of our Sunday evenings are spent at the lush green lawns of the Gandhi Smarak situated at the North Maharashtra University Campus. It is fun to enjoy the outdoor freshness and the activities of the children playing there.

One Sunday at the Smarak, I get talking to a family friend, Vinod Agrawal, a chartered accountant and a successful businessman. He asks me how I view the current recession. I tell him, 'I don't feel any recession. Recession is an excuse that many people give for their under-performance.'

After all, how many of us, at our scales, are truly affected by the global recession? In fact, my own business has grown! In our food-processing unit, we are undergoing an expansion. A lot of my clients are buying machines and also expanding capacities or upgrading to better technology. I know many friends who have either expanded or diversified. I see people busy preparing to ride the tide once the initial shake-up is over. Technology is cheap. Good and experienced manpower is in plenty. Suppliers want clients. It's time to lower your input costs.

I feel that because some of us don't want to stretch, reach out and make the effort, we find it simpler to blame the market and become the harbingers of doom, predicting further decline. I agree that there is a correction in the market but it is sector-specific. Real estate, leisure spending and so on are affected. But people are coming up with great ideas, and never-before offers. It has helped them become more cost-effective. Realtors are at least talking about low-cost housing. Many big groups have already launched such schemes.

Attending to pending work, sharpening the focus, becoming market-centric, customer-centric, working on efficient production methods, better financial management, working on the debtors, on manpower training... The intelligent people in industry are working on all these fronts to prepare for greater success when the situation improves.

So, get out of the negative spiral and shake the monster of recession off your necks. You will grow both personally and professionally by adopting better practices.

A crisis is a wonderful opportunity you cannot afford to miss!

Stones and Milestones

Obstacles are those frightful things you see
when you take your eyes off the goal.

—HANNAH MORE

If you find a pattern with no obstacles, it probably doesn't lead anywhere.

—FRANK A. CLARK

Sachin Tendulkar, the cricket legend, reached the immense milestone of 12,000 runs, and in a special interview after the day's play, Ravi Shastri asked him, 'How do you feel?'

In a remarkable statement, the Master Blaster said, 'You have ups and downs in your career. There are times when people throw stones at you. You have to convert them into milestones and proceed.'

There are bad patches in everyone's life. Jack Welch, Amitabh Bachchan, Steve Jobs, Diego Maradona, Dhirubhai Ambani, Abraham Lincoln—everyone has had to touch the bottom at least once in their lives. It is from this pit that they all surged up. Failed strategies transformed them. It was from the frustrations that a tough leader came alive.

Sunil Mittal, the magic man of the Bharti Airtel Group, once quoted words by Mahatma Gandhi that seemed appropriate to him in his fighting phase in the telecom industry. He said, 'At first people ignore you, then they laugh at you, then they fight you, and it is here that those who persist, and try hard with a lot of passion, eventually win!'

Sachin Tendulkar's expression of converting 'Stones into Milestones' also speaks of a proactive stand. Rather than worrying about a potential problem, think of how you can use it to your advantage and come up to make a mark, reach a milestone.

This 'Milestone' approach is what will make us look smartly towards failures.

In fact, in your failure is one more opportunity to make your mark, to establish a bigger milestone. Reinforcing your belief in your capabilities helps you grow from your mistakes. It gives you the wisdom and the strength to listen to your inner voice and fuels your passion to realize your dreams.

This 'Milestone' approach from the one and only Tendulkar is a great lesson to help you middle the ball no matter what googlies life throws at you.

Anxiety About Change

You have to stop in order to change direction.

—ERICH FROMM

There is nothing wrong with change, if it is in the right direction.

—WINSTON CHURCHILL

Recently, I was working as an associate for an international training firm to deliver a programme for a multinational bank. I was travelling to Delhi for the last phase of the briefing. I landed at the Delhi airport and walked through the long but extremely well-crafted Terminal 3 and booked myself on a prepaid taxi to Noida.

As we were leaving the main barricade of the airport, a young man asked the taxi driver if he would drop him to a metro railway station that was on the way. The taxi driver told me he knew the man, who worked for Air India, took my permission and then asked the man to join him in the front. Soon they were talking about the daily challenges they faced.

The Ministry of Civil Aviation had recently merged Indian Airlines, the domestic air travel company, with Air India, which used to operate international flights. The young man with us in the taxi worked in the ticketing section, and dealt directly with passengers. Of late, he said, he and his colleagues had been having a very difficult time. International flights operated late at night, and domestic flights from early morning till 11 p.m. Since the merger, there had been several occasions when passengers of domestic flights would find themselves dealing with the support staff of international flights, and vice versa. There was complete chaos, the young man said, and it was people like him who had to face the heat. His final comment was, 'The ministry really had no reason to merge the two operations. They take a major step like this just for the heck of it and create a mess. It's staff like us who suffer the consequences. What do ministers and bureaucrats know? Why did they have to do this?'

The man sounded frustrated that he had to manage a situation that, he felt, he had nothing to do with. Listening to him, I was thinking about the mood he might be projecting at the service desk, the most important point of contact for the passengers with the airline company. Honestly, for some years now the image of this particular airline had been of a slow, inefficient 'typical government' type. Now, the unhappiness of its employees, especially those who interacted with the company's clients, was probably making this aspect much worse.

Do we understand the importance of information in any change process and, more so, in a merger of two organizations?

It is well known that people, if left in doubt, get anxious. In the process of any radical change, the true facts, the reasons for and the importance of change, should be made very clear. It is imperative to reach out to everyone who will be affected by the change. Otherwise, there is anxiety, scepticism, insecurity, alienation and disconnectedness. All this leads inevitably to the negative spiral of energy drain and lack of enthusiasm. Once this happens in any organization, people are de-motivated, they look for other options and it becomes extremely difficult for the change leaders to create a positive momentum and lead the initiative.

A simple act of providing information about the intent of a merger and broadcasting it through all available means can help in an early buy-in among all stakeholders. The most important role of all managers before and during any process of change is to communicate with their teams, to reassure them and thus enlist their wholehearted support in the process. Many change initiatives fail and lose their visible benefits simply because people who initiate or carry out the change assume that the right information is reaching the concerned people and that everyone understands the need for it.

When you lead any change, big or small, professional or personal, in your office or in your home, please keep a very open channel of communication and proactively address everyone's concerns. The process of change will become less difficult for them and make the ride less bumpy for you.

After that taxi ride from the Delhi airport to Noida, I became conscious of the unspoken discomfort in my own office, which, too, was in the middle of an important change. I made some mental notes and called my manager to schedule a meeting with the concerned department heads.

The lift to an airport staff gave my change initiative a smooth take off!

Reinvent the Wheel

The riskiest thing we can do is just maintain the status quo.

—BOB IGER

The manager accepts the status quo; the leader changes it.

—WARREN G. BENNIS

I am in the middle of reading a beautiful book, *Creativity* by Alexander Hiam. The copy was gifted to me by a very sincere, meticulous, nature-loving chartered accountant and fellow Rotarian, Anil Shah.

One of the reasons Hiam cites for people not developing creativity is 'failure to tolerate creative behaviour.' Let me quote some lines from his book:

'How many bosses would give a word of encouragement to a subordinate if they were to come upon him sitting at his desk, chair tipped back, foot resting on an open drawer and staring into space with an abstract expression on his face? They'd be far more likely to ask him what the hell he's doing, and if the unfortunate replies, "Thinking," he'd probably be advised to stop thinking and get back to work.' (Hiam takes this example from another book, Elliot Carlisle's *Mac*.)

Can you connect with this situation? When did you last let your co-worker wander astray, yet not discipline him or laugh at him?

Do you tell your son to stop tapping his feet and fingers when food is being served at the dining table?

Do you tell your daughter that she is irresponsible when she cuts up the newspaper before you can read it?

Do you get annoyed at your sister's son because he opens up the expensive airplane model you've just gifted him?

Do you allow your co-workers to experiment with a new idea, even if it means some financial loss to your office?

Do you let the grandchild of the house try his hands with crayons or pencil on the walls of the house?

Learn to nurture the creative streak in the people around you.

Believe in their 'foolishness', enjoy their untidy mannerisms, and tolerate their need to do things differently.

If some people hadn't questioned the status quo and reinvented the wheel, your car would move on a cross-section of a trunk with a hole bored in it. It took 4,500 years of experimenting for the wheel to become what it is today—a flexible rim with spokes running to a solid hub.

Would you still say 'Do not reinvent the wheel?'

Doing Things Differently:
Customer Success

Until you know what it takes to achieve success from your customers'
perspective, you will just waste valuable time…'

–JASON WHITEHEAD

We know of concepts like 'Customer satisfaction' and 'Customer relationships'. Today, leaders and industry experts are talking about 'Customer success'.

The concept is simple yet extremely powerful—unless you do not help your customer become successful, he will not buy your product or service.

Let me give you an example.

Consider the investment services. Why would your client invest with you?

You may give the routine answers: 'I give him better service' or 'My investments fetch better returns' or 'I have good information on the investment bankers' or 'Your money is safe with us' or, 'We truly care…' And so on.

None of these things truly matter in the end. Customer success does.

The concept of customer success, applied, is something like this:

In the first place, an investor will invest only when he has a surplus. So, if you help him increase his earnings and hence the surplus, you will benefit. Or, if you, as a raw material supplier, are able to deliver a better yield or enhanced quality that adds to the bottom line of your client, you become a respectable supplier.

Wouldn't we all prefer a person who helps us earn more money through his services rendered to us?

So, what can you do to make your customer more successful?

What can you do to help him grow his business?

What strategies if implemented by your customer can help him go to the next level?

Always remember—your growth to the next level is dependent on your customer's growth. Can you work differently to ensure this?

Atmosphere Counts

More often than not, things and people are as they appear.

—MALCOLM FORBES

Jiten Shende, the then Chief Executive Officer of G.G. Dandekar Machine Works, the largest manufacturer of the latest machinery for rice milling in India, is an unusual man, who has displayed tremendous guts in transforming his business. He has risen to unique corporate success from the cricket field, successfully applying the rules of the game to the corporate world, always working on the basics.

In the mornings, he walks to the desks of all his executives, including the juniormost officers. He talks to them with full energy and enthusiasm, which naturally, is contagious. It sets the tone for the day.

He shifted his office from the mill town of Bhiwandi on the outskirts of Mumbai Andheri, a suburb of the city, because of a very simple yet powerful belief he had: the atmosphere counts.

The old manufacturing site in Bhiwandi was not the ideal place for the sales office, which, being where it was, lacked a truly corporate identity. The rooms were too large and old-style, the tables and chairs a little too old; voices echoed in the large space, it was often hot and humid and the energy levels were low. Jiten decided to shift his sales staff to the new premises, very close to his market, knowing that the company needed to work on the top line really hard. The neat cabinets in the new office, the partitioned yet open office cubicles, the white blinds on the windows, the soothing blue sofa and chairs in the waiting room, the books on technology and Robin Sharma's motivational books on the bookshelves—all of these things created the perfect ambience.

This was not about an expensive décor. It was about something far more substantial. The setting of our work place makes a difference in the attitude with which we go about our work.

I spoke to the sales people in Jiten's new office shortly after the shift and I could feel a different vibration in them, a new energy. Although they were travelling for about 50 minutes extra to reach the new office, their performance and, more importantly, their outlook had changed.

I learnt an important lesson from this example—the ambience counts.

Playing with the right colours, setting and layout of your work place has a direct effect on how you work.

Apply this to your staff's work place as well. If they are not feeling as energized as they should, try to add a little something to their setting. May be a plant near the workstation. Or a painting or photograph on the wall, a vinyl flooring carpet, some soft music....All of this is inexpensive but adds value your office. The office will not just look good, but feel good.

So many of us end up spending a packet on expensive décor merely to impress visitors. I know of people who go to the extent of buying gold-plated taps for their washrooms. What is the purpose here? It is useless trying to dazzle people—mainly outsiders to your work and business—with such extravagance.

It is external gratification, at best. True and lasting satisfaction is completely an internal state of mind.

Discipline or Compliance?

The more decisions that you are forced to make alone,
the more you are aware of your freedom to choose.

—THORNTON WILDER

Discipline without freedom is tyranny. Freedom without discipline is chaos.

—CULLEN HIGHTOWER

Recently, I read a fantastic book called *Managing Radical Change* by the great teacher of strategic management at the London Business School, Professor Sumanthra Ghoshal, Gita Piramal and Christopher Bartlett.

In the organizational context, the authors have made a wonderful differentiation between 'discipline' and 'compliance'. On the face of it, compliance seems to be a product of laws, rules and regulations: 'You have to do it this way!' Compliance has an outside-in effect—it is about *imposing* things on people—and hence there is the urge to challenge and defy it. Don't we all like to break rules, just for the thrill? That's the effect of compliance.

On the other hand, discipline comes by virtue of an inner commitment: 'I must do the task in this way; I would like to.' It is an inside-out approach and hence creates the urge to stick by it. Even forced stimuli can have this effect. It runs on the principle of the long-term, because you have fundamentally accepted those 'rules' or 'way of working'—they are rules you have voluntarily accepted, they are not imposed on you.

For example, imagine yourself as the owner or general manager of a factory. You make a rule that no one working in the factory will chew gutka. You enforce the rule strictly and soon after you don't see anyone chewing gutka. But you still find gutka wrappers lying in the premises. Clearly, the rule has worked only to an extent—no one will openly chew gutka but they will in secret. This is mere compliance.

Discipline would result if the workers understood the rule and followed it because they wanted to. This would happen if it was explained to them how, by giving up the habit of chewing gutka, they would be improving their health and saving money which could be used for their children's higher education or marriage.

To take another example: A company gives its managers two days' leave every year for CSR (corporate social responsibility) work. Chances are, the managers will manufacture proof of having done CSR work that they never really did, or if they do any such work, they'll probably do it half-heartedly. Instead, the company could take the managers to an institution for physically or mentally challenged people and let them see how even small acts can change the lives of those people. The managers would also experience the satisfaction of doing something that brings tangible benefits to their fellow human beings. Once they realize this, they will be invested in CSR work and do it regularly of their own free will.

The Discipline of Freedom

Those who expect to reap the blessing of freedom must undertake to support it.

—THOMAS PAINE

Freedom without obligation is democracy.

—EARL RINEY

Whether it is a business organization or a civic set-up, Freedom needs to be disciplined with Responsibility.

All of us want freedom: the freedom to act, to speak, to live, to enjoy, to follow our heart, to work for the fulfilment of our personal needs.

But do we act responsibly towards this freedom?

Freedom to do what we want is an invitation into the domain of selfishness, and we do visit it quite often. It is inevitable. But greatness is achieved only when we enjoy this freedom with an acute sense of the need to respect the space, lifestyles, well-being and freedom of others in our organization, and in society in general.

We may be politically correct, but are we also morally correct?

A sales representative, for example, makes the 15 calls he is required to make in a day, and claims that he has done his job, done it perfectly. But how many of those calls generated business?

Many business decisions that seem to be correct for your own organization or industry can have negative consequences for society or the world at large. What is profitable for you may add to pollution or global warming, for instance, or the advertising campaign for one of your products may, in fact, be hurting the pride and self-respect of a particular group or community. The net result, then, destroys rather than adds value.

There have been numerous high-profile cases of morally wrong means adopted by businesses in pursuit of higher profits or expansion: Enron's accounting fraud, the Lehman Brothers' crisis, the Rajat Gupta affair, the Subrata Roy case.

The corporate world has seriously started revisiting the idea of profit and success, favouring long-term, all-round gains over short-term individual gains. Coke and Pepsi, for instance, had to acknowledge the possible harmful effects that indiscriminate use of sweetened aerated drinks can have on people's health. They introduced diet versions of their drinks, and have also added fruit juices in their product line. They realized the need to respect the consumers' freedom to have alternatives to regular aerated drinks.

Generators were a huge need due to frequent power cuts, but they caused significant sound pollution. Few manufacturers acted responsibly. So sound-proof cabinets had to be made compulsory for generators.

Plastic bags, though convenient, are an environmental hazard. Paper bags are the better option, and responsible businesses are working to promote the use of alternatives to plastic. D Mart, for example, advocates that you to carry a shopping bag from home; else they charge ₹ 3.50 for a bag.

Fast foods have long been known to be unhealthy. Many governments and some industries are now promoting healthy eating habits and the use of organic food products.

Enron had to pay the price for its unethical behaviour in the Dabhol power plant project.

There is, of course, a long way to go, but the process has begun. The best regarded and most enduring businesses, entrepreneurs, managers and individuals will be those who understand that control and a tight rein has a balancing effect to the flight of the kite of freedom, which is essential. Otherwise it would be very difficult to avoid a nose-dive. Act with freedom definitely; but always ensure that you are not violating the space or undermining the freedom and well-being of others.

To respect the needs and freedom of others is the unwritten law that governs our pursuit and enjoyment of our personal freedom.

Apply this as much to your family life as to your professional life. Certain values must be protected for a healthy family life, and this may require that the freedom of some members of the family is disciplined. This is best done voluntarily—as you voluntarily restrict some of your freedom, encourage other individuals in the family to also do this of their own accord. The sense of satisfaction you earn when you give up a little of what is precious to you, especially your freedom, for the sake of others elevates you not only in the eyes of those who benefit from this, but also in your own eyes!

The Day After

It is better to have a hen tomorrow than an egg today.

—THOMAS FULLER

When you arrive at your future, will you blame your past?

—ROBERT HALF

The future is purchased by the present.

—SAMUEL JOHNSON

I've got back to writing after a gap. I've restarted writing on a good day, the birthday of my elder brother Kishor, and also that of my friend Nandu, whose remark made me think about and adopt 'slow management'.

My brother is foresight personified. His anticipation and planning for the future, particularly financial planning, is great. At the time when funds are surplus, he starts thinking of his grandchildren and their growing years. Rather than spending on material things, his priority is to invest for the future in insurance, mutual funds, or gold and precious material. I sometimes feel uncomfortable at the thought of someone not enjoying the present and worrying about the future. But Kishor, with his worldly knowledge, proves me wrong, and I'm thankful for what he has taught me through this.

When I think about it carefully, I realize that while my brother does maintain a balance between the present and the future, his tilt is always towards the day after. This has a tremendous benefit in the sense of security, some insurance against the unseen. Financial security for the days ahead keeps you calm and relaxed. It could be anything—your child's education, your health, the marriage of your niece, the health insurance of your domestic help...

Building up of capital in your personal accounts, which increases your credibility with financial institutions, also requires foresight, planning and, of course, sacrifice of material happiness for the short-term.

And the sacrifice is worth it. Don't you feel great about the land that your grandfather purchased years ago and is worth a few millions today? Or the commercial property your father invested in, in your name, when you were in kindergarten and where your business is now flourishing? Or the farmland, an ancestral holding, that your parents and grandparents did not sell off and which is now so sought after by an international hotel chain that is keen to develop a resort? Your forefathers sacrificed some material happiness in their 'today' to make your future better.

Think. Create a balance between today and tomorrow, but with a bias for the day after. Money matters! Especially when you need it badly but do not have sufficient resources to earn it—your physical resources being the foremost. There are no guarantees in life, so be wise and look to the future.

Action Words

Words are the most powerful drug used by mankind.

—RUDYARD KIPLING

Words are loaded pistols.

—JEAN-PAUL SARTRE

My friend Deepak Sanghavi, a man with phenomenal initiative and appetite for risk-taking, is the Managing Director of a company called Nilons. This, and his great equation with his dynamic CEO, Rajeev Agrawal, has ensured that Nilons is going great guns in the FMCG (Fast-moving Consumer Goods) foods business.

When they planned for the future some years ago, their vision was to become a 500-crore organization and grow at 70 per cent CAGR (Compound Annual Growth Rate) for three years in a row. But their growth plans were hampered by the recession in 2008. That was also the time when, only a couple of months earlier, they'd had foreign investment made in their group. Together with the new partners, Deepak and Rajeev had made certain growth commitments, unaware of the creeping recession that was unanticipated by almost everyone globally.

As market forces crushed the economy, they had all the reasons, logical and convincing, to expect zero growth in the first half of the financial year. The new investors, too, in the light of the general business climate having gone out of control, accepted this sorry state. But, insane as it may seem—and as it may have appeared to their own investors—the duo declared that they must settle for nothing less than 25 per cent growth in the year, which meant it would have to be 50 per cent in the remaining six months (for an annual average of 25 per cent).

The mood was not at all encouraging. Negativity of market conditions had already set in among members of the sales team. But a huge action plan was charted out that listed the top four leaders of the organization, including Deepak and Rajeev, meeting the entire market personally; a 50 per cent increase in work time for the sales staff; 60-second decision-making initiatives by the leaders, and so forth. There was a great obsession to 'execute'.

The team travelled 28 days a month, 15 to 18 hours a day were spent on the field, and the entire exercise went on for six months.

This operation was named 'Mahayudh' (the Great Battle) so that action would be seen and felt at every level of the management. And things started to happen.

I am more than convinced that the word 'Mahayudh' had resonance among all the staff. They understood that as in a great war, this was a matter of life and death, of their very survival. Everyone in the organization, then, was highly motivated. They all raised the bar, broke out of their comfort zones, sweated it out, combed the market, added new channels, came out with innovative sales schemes and literally fought back like warriors—striking, saving, conquering people's minds.

Sales grew by about 46 per cent in three months.

Whenever there was doubt or fatigue, that one word,

'Mahayudh', transformed attitudes all over again. There was, once again, an adrenaline rush, and everyone was inspired to act—hard and positively.

A single action word or phrase can make a clear difference. I, for instance, sign off my correspondence by adding to my name the words 'Celebrating Life'. It is a great reminder to embrace life.

It is a well-known fact that thoughts create words, and words drive action. Having a great action word acts both on your thoughts and, thereby, on your action. And actions create habits that build character.

Make your own list of power-packed words and phrases and experience a quantum leap in your life. You will not merely live, but thrive. Energy words create a chain reaction. Use the power of words to ignite the fuel to perform. It works—and works really well!

Here, then, are some Action Words and Phrases:

1. Celebrate Life
2. Wow! (My exclamation after I get out of bed every morning.)
3. Happy morning! (Instead of Good morning!)
4. Excited to be Alive! (a mantra often used by Mahatria Rā of Infinitheism)
5. Mahayudh.
6. HallaBol! (Another initiative by Nilons to induce a market-capture operation.)
7. Changing Lives.
8. Great Place to Work.
9. Just Do it.
10. Axing Business.

11. Aage Badho!
12. Dream for the Sun.
13. Junoon.
14. Josh.
15. Fly High.
16. RISE.
17. Growth.
18. Leading by Choice.
19. Servant Leadership.
20. Service above Self (An award in the rotary world).
21. Manking is our Business (A rotary theme).
22. No pain (The auto suggestion in a boxing ring).

What Not to Do

What you don't do is as important as what you do. Here is a list of daily chores I have consciously decided not to do. Instead, I have efficient staff handling all this:

- Pick up my phone when I'm having my dinner or lunch.
- Make my railway reservations.
- Deal about advances to my factory staff.
- Pay electricity, mobile and telephone bills. (I don't even check them.)
- Make power-point presentations.
- Feed data in my computer.
- Maintain hardware/software.
- Drive my car.
- Pay my insurance, taxes, sales tax returns.
- Work with my chartered accountant on tax planning.
- Plan and make loan repayments, if any.
- Buy routine machines and consumables.
- Work on design details of layouts for my clients.
- Visit banks for monetary transactions.
- Pay the cable TV agent.
- Make appointments for business meetings.
- Coordinate with the maintenance guys of EPABX, white goods, water purifier, electrical fittings and appliances, plumbing, cooking gas, and so on.

- ▶ Make hotel reservations.
- ▶ Write business letters, quotations.
- ▶ Send routine greetings or condolence telegrams.
- ▶ Read junk mail.
- ▶ Go shopping, just to pass the time.

And then there are things that I will never, never do. And no one can fill in for me, either. Unless I'm travelling, for instance, I will never miss lunch and dinner with my daughter.

Time is precious, don't waste it on things someone else can do just as well or even better than you.

Equally, there are some things that only you can do, no one can do them for you. And you need to ensure you are free to do these.

COMMUNICATION
The Art of Living Together

The Way of Kids

We try to make our children become more like us, instead of trying to become more like them, with the result that we pick up none of their good traits, and they pick up most of our bad ones.

—SYDNEY J. HARRIS

My friend, Deepak Sanghavi, and his gracious wife, Ritu, have a lovely son, Sanskar, aged two and a half, who attends Wisdom, the play school run by my wife. Recently, Ritu shared with us a story about Sanskar.

Ritu had gone to visit a family friend and taken Sanskar along. The little boy played on the lawns while his mother was inside the house, chatting. When it was time to leave, she went out to fetch Sanskar, and when she found him, she noticed that he was barefoot. Believing that the boy had tossed his shoes off somewhere, Ritu began looking for them in the house, under the sofa, in the balcony, on the staircase, out on the lawns. When her search yielded nothing, she turned to her son and asked him why he'd been irresponsible and misplaced his shoes.

Little Sanskar then took his mother by the hand to the shoe rack near the entrance to the house, where he had kept his shoes neatly. It was a habit he had picked up in his play school.

Ritu was both pleased and humbled. She regretted having thought that her child had been careless. He had put his shoes in the right place—it was she who had first made the wrong assumption and then wasted time looking for them in the wrong places.

Don't we older people almost always presume that our little ones are not capable of acting responsibly without our instruction? Don't we always teach them our ways, convinced that we adults know best?

We want our children to live our autobiography—walk in our footsteps, or follow our dreams. We don't believe that they are competent and creative enough to find newer and better ways to do things. We rarely want to listen to them. In the process, we could be passing on our wrong beliefs and irrational thoughts to them, filling their clean minds with our own mental detritus.

The next time, pause before you judge and label your little ones. Learn to trust them more than you do; listen to them. It will help them grow and develop their own vision for the world, which may be a better one than ours.

And once you have done this—once you have trained yourself to learn from your youngest, most taken-for-granted companions—you will be a wiser person yourself, willing and able to learn from everyone you work with or meet socially or even encounter very briefly.

Simple and Effective Concern

It is not where you serve, but how you serve.

–J. RUBIN CLARK

It was a very busy week. I had back-to-back speaking engagements. In the middle of this, my son was on a school-hunting mission for his class 11 admissions. He had decided to opt out of engineering and medicine and pursue economics instead. We wanted a school environment and not a regular college where he would stay in a private hostel. We decided on a school in Bengaluru, and were allotted a day for the school visit, interview and admission tests.

It was a last-moment travel plan. We managed to book ourselves on a Spice Jet flight to Bengaluru. We had a busy day ahead—visit the school, about 65 km from the airport, complete the long agenda there, and travel back to the airport for the evening return flight.

The attendants on the flight served us some sandwiches and juices for breakfast. The courtesy and efficiency were a welcome beginning to our otherwise hectic schedule. But the best was yet to come.

A short while before we began our descent, the attendants went down the aisle collecting the used plates in a clean garbage bag. What struck me was the announcement that supported this mundane act: 'Being on time is an important virtue. Please help us to be on time by dropping your used plates in the bags. This will help us to clean the aircraft faster after it reaches Bengaluru and let your fellow passengers flying with us from Bengaluru be on time.'

There was so much forethought, planning and concern in those lines.

The flight was to land at about 9 a.m. We were in a rush to make it to the school on time and finish all formalities in the few hours we'd have in Bengaluru. The airhostess began to make the normal pre-landing announcements, telling us about the weather in the city, expressing her gratitude to all passengers for choosing the flight—all the things we seldom pay attention to. But there was more than mere routine stuff. That, and the manner in which the lady delivered the lines had me hooked despite my anxiety about our whistle-stop school visit:

'Please close your laptops and do not forget to save your work. Please check your belongings and memory sticks you might have put on the seat or the side pockets.'

The valuable emotional connect of 'we are concerned' was clear in every single announcement, both in the script and the delivery.

For the people who wrote those lines and the staff who spoke them, several times a day, this was routine. And yet it had meaning each time, it was as effective as it was simple. For me, this was a lesson in day-to-day communication—how something routine done with thoughtfulness and professionalism with a personal touch can be valuable. For my son and I it was a great way to start our busy day in Bengaluru.

Thanks, Spice Jet.

Customer Complaints

Anger is never without a reason, but seldom with a good one.

—BENJAMIN FRANKLIN

The electricity board in Maharashtra is under huge stress. The gap between demand and supply is constantly getting wider. The state government has some ambitious projects, and it buys power from neighbouring states, but despite all its efforts, the crisis continues. People in urban regions have to face power cuts for almost six hours a day, and in rural areas it can get as bad as 12 to 16 hours a day without electricity.

Naturally, it is a tough time for the wiremen and junior engineers who man the substations and attend to telephone calls from irate customers.

We, as a training agency, have been working with the electricity board, most closely with the wiremen and middle-level engineers, for almost three years. One of our focus areas in the training is customer complaints.

One day, I went on a visit to the Mehrun region of the Jalgaon city office. Some residential areas there were experiencing power cuts well beyond the board's declared schedule for load-shedding. As I entered the substation, I saw an angry-looking man park his two-wheeler. He rushed into the office soon after me. You could tell from a distance that he was in a temper.

Sensing a turbulent situation, the wireman immediately stood up, smiled at the man and said, 'Namaskar.' The customer was in no mood to reciprocate the wireman's greeting and told him in a voice dripping with scorn, 'Are you aware that we've been calling you for days? Do you have any idea why? We've been complaining but no one seems to be concerned. So I had to come over here in person!'

The wireman, an experienced man, looked at the customer, leaned forward and held his hand. And with seemingly genuine concern he said, smiling, 'Thank you. How would our office have been honoured by your presence otherwise?'

The customer's anger melted away. He suddenly felt important and smiled back. He then went on to ask, albeit in a much calmer voice, what could be done to resolve the matter.

I had witnessed a genuine lesson in converting an angry customer and bringing him over to your side, and then making him feel that he was important and valued in spite of the complaint that he had.

I could see that our training was probably working and the electricity board was acquiring the tools to handle the day-to-day stressful moments.

Disagreement

The aim of an argument is not victory but progress.

—OSCAR WILDE

This quote on the notice board outside my son's school dormitory caught my attention one day.

Why and how do we argue?

- Is it out of resentment or out of a need to explore and understand?
- Are we interested only in defeating the other person and negating his or her viewpoint?
- Are we flexible or do we want to be rigid simply to protect our ego?
- Do we listen attentively or are we busy preparing ourselves to respond even more strongly to the point being made by the other party? (We often have this notion that when we speak loudly, or shout, our point will be accepted.)

The very basis of a democratic set-up calls for constructive opposition; else we can never grow and evolve.

How do you disagree?

Answering this one question has helped me greatly to communicate better. I never have a monologue. I listen, so that I can understand. I'm able to receive ideas, comments, solutions, criticism and observations in the correct perspective. It helps me work better, and to evolve as a person. After all, evolution is survival of the fittest.

The viewpoints in a team vary, yet there is a need to function together, following certain set norms and procedures. It is imperative that matters of great importance are discussed at length before the actual compliance. A healthy discussion not only helps refine the subject but each person in the team also develops a sense of ownership and then compliance transcends to discipline, or rather self-discipline.

There might be certain norms on which it is difficult to arrive at a 100 per cent consensus. But the fact that there has been enough real and serious discussion reduces the intensity of disagreement.

Work with everyone in your team, invite healthy discussions; they will feel invested in the enterprise and you will have a disciplined, committed team.

Agree to Disagree

A long dispute means that both the parties are wrong.

—VOLTAIRE

Men are not against you, they're merely for themselves.

—GENE FOWLER

There is a sea of difference between 'I agree to disagree' and 'I disagree'.

The first is Proactive, the second Reactive.

Agreeing to disagree is a mature way of respecting the freedom of thought of the other individual. When you agree to disagree, you have given enough thought to the other person's point of view; you have tried to correlate that with your own beliefs and then have decided on the disagreement.

'I disagree', on the other hand, is usually about defending a position simply to avoid the discomfort of losing. And when that happens, you have closed your channel of receptivity. When you become emotionally attached to a particular viewpoint, or when it becomes a matter of pride, then logic or reason stop aiding your thought process. You tend to get carried away and feel a high level of 'over-involvement'.

A word of caution: Many a time, people use the first phrase—'agree to disagree'—without really feeling that way, simply because it sounds better. They agree to disagree without any serious thought or respect for the opposing point of view. This, too, is the result of a closed channel of receptivity. It's also quite possible that because they have not understood or applied enough reason, some people agree to disagree simply to avoid getting into someone's bad books.

But one must always understand that *disagreement does not imply enmity.* Life would be monotonous, and indeed poorer, if there was no difference between the two.

Think about it. Could breakthroughs or scientific inventions ever occur if everyone accepted the status quo? If no one questioned, argued or debated? A significant development occurs only when someone disagrees with the accepted norms, with the done thing. We need to challenge the norms, question the premises.

However, blind rejection or unhealthy dislike of what one questions or disagrees with, yields nothing of value. There can, then, be no breakthrough or progress.

We can learn to disagree—without getting obsessive about our point of view and without letting negativity creep into a disagreement.

Wired to Disconnect

I have three chairs in my house; one for solitude, two for friendship and three for society.

—HENRY DAVID THOREAU

I was travelling back from Pune after a programme with Hindustan Petroleum Corporation Ltd. I love such train journeys. My father used to say, 'If you want to learn about people, travel in trains, in buses. You will learn true-life lessons.' The sharing of experiences along with pickle or mint chocolates with a co-passenger is a real mental feast.

But of late these journeys have become lonely affairs. People are immersed in their laptops or i-Pods or mobiles. We seem to connect with virtual world and not the real one. We do not even bother to smile at a co-passenger, forget about asking his name and profession.

Just about 12 or 15 years back, when India was not so gadget-obsessed, a friend of mine travelling by train struck up a conversation with a gentleman who later became his father-in-law. Two families had come together. This wasn't unusual. Not so long ago, so many business or other relationships would gather momentum on such journeys. It was a great way to network.

Today, you are made to listen to the songs on a smart phone

belonging to the college girl in the next compartment, or the electronic noise of Game Boy that the young boy of eight on the berth above you has been playing for almost two hours without pause. Or you are distracted by the loud Hollywood images flashing on the screen of a co-traveller's Mac Book even as you are desperately trying to catch some sleep after a long day. Everyone is disconnected in the social context, limiting himself or herself only to his or her virtual reach.

Isn't it a better idea to exchange live, real smiles with your colleague sitting in the next cubicle, or a co-passenger on a journey, than to exchange a 'smiley' with an unknown chat friend in cyberspace?

I have always thought that travelling is a time you can use to play a board game with your children, teach them to draw a cartoon, play antakshari or discuss a science issue with them, invite them to enjoy a breathtaking view, help them interact and negotiate with a passing hawker, make them understand the value of compassion to the little boy who just cleaned your compartment for the leftover contents of a tiffin box...

So much to learn and to teach, instead of shutting yourself off from the real world for the sake of the virtual connections.

Relationships

'Only connect.'

—E.M. FORSTER

Biscuit Companions

Thank the Lord that you can give, instead of depending on others to give you.

—ANONYMOUS

One morning, I decided to take a long walk in the park at Mumbai's Bandra-Kurla complex.

There weren't many people in the park that day. After a strenuous 45-minute walk, I decided to rest for a while and have a cup of chai or coffee. I found a small tea stall, and as I waited for my 'peshal' (special) coffee, I noticed a lady of about 40, a little plump, not obviously well to do, probably a clerk in some government organization, talking to a couple of stray dogs affectionately. There were three or four of them, wagging their tails and jumping around her. She called them by their pet names—Chhotu, Rani, Jimmy.

I smiled at the lady and asked if they were her biscuit companions. She nodded. Then an errand boy from the tea stall came up to her and handed her some freshly baked local cookies. She served these to the stray dogs. She did not throw the cookies on the ground but fed the dogs with her hand. To one she said, 'Will you eat the whole biscuit?' and knowing that the dog probably would not, she broke a biscuit and gave it half.

All the strays had their breakfast and then followed the lady like old friends, presumably to her office, where, perhaps, they would wait for her till the evening when she would finish work and they would walk her home.

The tea-stall owner told me this was a daily routine. I wondered about the expenses involved. It was obvious that the lady was from the lower end of the city's middle class. And yet she spent—by a rough estimate—at least ten rupees every day on the stray dogs.

Mumbai may be money-obsessed, but its heart was very much in the right place.

In my mind I thanked the lady for the act of Giving. My coffee tasted unusually 'peshal' that day.

The next morning I met the lady again, at the same tea stall, and got talking to her. I gathered that she was involved with the catering services of MMRDA (Mumbai Metropolitan Region Development Authority). I also gathered that she spent twice the amount that I had estimated on feeding her canine friends.

The Side Effects of Giving

A tree is known by its fruit; a man by his deeds. A good deed is never lost; he who sows courtesy reaps friendship, and he who plants kindness gathers love.

—SAINT BASIL

All the world's religions say that we must give in abundance to the less privileged. The psychological equivalent of giving materially is a compassionate attitude. Empathy and compassion are considered great emotions, and they in turn trigger happiness and positivity in us. It has been affirmed by PET and MRI scans that compassion activates the left hemisphere of the neo-cortex, which is the seat for happy feelings.

Simply put, when you give, you are as much a beneficiary as the one who receives your help.

Haven't you felt elated when you donated blood, bought a cup of chai for a beggar, shared your last bit of mango with your friend's little daughter, served food in the home for the destitute, given blankets to the homeless, distributed medicines in the slums, taken loads of daily needs to earthquake-affected areas?

Giving has great side effects. What is more valuable than a feeling of well-being and peace with oneself?

Keep giving.

The Hindu *Shastras* prescribe three ways of giving: Tan

(body), Mann (Mind) and Dhan (Money)—that is, through physical acts, thoughts or ideas, and money.

Make your choice and see a change in your life. Giving has a profound effect on your whole being!

Saying Sorry

Sorry doesn't take things back, but it pushes things forward.
It bridges the gap. Sorry is a sacrament. It's an offering. A gift.

—CRAIG SILVEY

Raju is our dhobi who collects our clothes from home, irons them and brings them back, crisp and neatly folded, in a day or two. The most critical task is of keeping the account of the clothes he takes and the cost of ironing each piece of clothing—tallying the number of trousers, shirts, T-shirts, jeans, pyjamas, kurtas, sarees; and all of them further classified by size. It's a herculean task to receive the clothes the dhobi brings back and then tally them. Ultimately, my wife has turned to tallying only the total number. That's the best we can do, especially in a joint family where clothes of more than eight people are dealt with.

After the sorting of the respective clothes, each individual then checks his or her clothes and if there's an unfamiliar shirt or saree, the dhobi is ticked off—'Raju, *tum dekh-ke kapde layaa karo*' (Raju, check the clothes before you get them)—and he merrily ignores the half-hearted reprimand and goes on his way.

One particular day we had three items that were unidentified, We thought they could be our son's, but when he returned he said they weren't his. My wife, who had had a pretty tough day in her school, called up Raju. She yelled at him for the confusion and his increasing carelessness. She told him it was getting really painful to maintain his account. She was angry and she showed it.

Soon after this, I asked my son if the clothes belonged to a friend of his who had stayed with us a few days back. My son took a photo of the clothes with his phone and sent it to his friend for identification. The friend got back to us. The clothes were indeed his. My wife and I looked at each other; it was now clear who had been 'careless'.

My wife's biggest virtue is her purity of thought. The fact that she had reprimanded Raju unfairly this time made her uncomfortable. That night, after dinner, we went out for a drive. After a couple of silent minutes she picked up her cell phone and called up Raju. She apologized for firing him badly, explained what had happened and accepted that she was the one at fault. Raju, who obviously wasn't expecting this, was touched by her words and said, 'Bhabhiji, you think a lot about other people. Someone like you will never think ill of another. You don't have to apologize.'

Relieved after the call, my wife said, 'Take me to Domino's. I barely had anything for dinner, thinking of what I'd said to Raju and feeling guilty.'

It was a new lesson for me. When you make a mistake, never hide it. Do yourself a favour—own up and say sorry.

Shabaree

There is no need for temples; no need for complicated philosophy. Our own brain, our own heart is our temple; the philosophy is kindness.

—THE DALAI LAMA

Kindness is the golden chain by which society is bound together.

—GOETHE

A part of kindness consists in giving people more than they deserve.

—JOSEPH JOUBERT

Most of us have heard of the great epic *Ramayana*. Many of us have read a version of it, or watched its TV adaptation. There's a story in it that is a wonderful illustration of empathy. It is the story of Shabaree.

Prabhu Ram Chandra, during his fourteen-year exile in the forest, came to the ashram of an old woman called Shabaree. She had been expecting him, and had kept a bowl of berries in anticipation of his visit. A great devotee of Ram, she wanted to serve him only the tastiest and the sweetest fruits, so she tasted each berry before offering it to her idol. Some of Ram's companions objected, and advised him not to eat the berries that had been defiled by Shabaree. 'What kind of host are you'? they said. But Ram ignored them and ate every fruit that Shabaree gave him, savouring it and showing respect for her deep care and devotion.

This is true empathy—respecting the feelings of another and reciprocating a genuine act of concern or gratitude with a similar act. By doing this, you say, 'Thank you. I feel your feelings.'

This requires humility, great sensitivity and truthfulness. That is why empathy is difficult to practise. We usually practise it only when it is convenient. And then, too, it would be sympathy, where you start living in the other's world but are unable to reach out and make a difference. Empathy is different.

Let me explain. Sympathy is walking in another man's shoes forever—your experiences and his become the same, the worlds you inhabit are the same. This can be a handicap—you can share his pain but you can't help him. Empathy, on the other hand, is walking in another man's shoes for some time, sharing his pain and understanding it, then getting out of those shoes and doing something for him.

The challenge for us is to feel the pain of that shoe bite while walking in our own shoes. This requires some practice, but the effort is worth it. Empathy makes the lives of our fellow human beings, of all living beings, better, and therefore it improves our own life—our home, our business, our society.

Indifference

The opposite of love is not hate, but indifference.

What a powerful phrase this is! And so true.

In business organizations, social circles or families, the pain people feel because of indifference is all-pervasive.

Just think of those moments when the person you value or look up to just walks away with a cold look, without a word or any expression, as if you don't matter.

Maybe he was your teacher whom you respected the most but who put you down for some misdemeanour on your part or simply because someone else was his favourite. Or your mother, without whose lullaby you could not sleep, but who wouldn't sing to you because you stole that two-rupee coin for a chocolate. Or your father who doesn't talk to you because he felt cheated when he saw you smoking by the corner of the street. Or your wife who was hurt by your behaviour, your son or daughter whose birthday you missed while on your sales tour… You wish they would all be angry with you; the silence with which they turn away from you is unbearable.

Or think of a colleague who felt backstabbed when you got promoted instead of him…You expected him to hate you. But he did not. He simply did not think you were valuable enough to be hated. What he felt was indifference. And you could not stand it.

In fact, in hatred, the person has a strong feeling for you, which says, 'You have hurt me, disappointed me.' That is the pain of someone you love or trust not reposing love and confidence in you, and that pain and humiliation becomes hatred. So when someone hates you, you know that you meant something to the person, or you still mean something to him. But indifference is about a total lack of emotional connection. Humans have an emotional connection even to material things. In this case, you do not even have mere material value to the person whom you have wronged, or the person whom you like or respect but who doesn't like you or respect you back.

Know this, and you will understand better the big losses in your relationships, whether in your personal or professional life. It is indifference, not hatred for or an active dislike towards someone, that reduces the social value of an individual to negative.

And we humans are still social animals.

Trust

You may be deceived if you trust too much,
but you will live in torment if you do not trust enough.

—FRANK CRANE

Skepticism is slow suicide.

—RALPH WALDO EMERSON

I had just completed a programme with one of the Rotary clubs in Maharashtra. My taxi driver had left, due to an emergency, and I had to take the State Transport Bus at 5 the next morning. My nephew, Amit, dropped me at the bus depot. I took a window seat and waited for the bus to start.

Looking out, I saw an autorickshaw arrive at the side of the bus stand, zoom round our bus and come to an abrupt halt. The autorickshaw driver jumped out and extracted small parcels carrying the morning newspapers to be distributed to the nearby villages. The bus would deliver them. Dropping about 20-odd packets, the autowala zoomed out of the stand.

No delivery challan, no confirmation from any authority, no checking, no verbal confirmation. The entire transaction was based purely on trust! Every day this autorickshaw man dropped these parcels to be delivered, certain that they would be delivered, though there was no contract, no record, no guarantee.

Think over this and you will see that the foundation of

every human enterprise, of the act of living itself, is trust.

We trust that we shall be alive tomorrow and hence pray to the Almighty the previous night for a prosperous day ahead.

We trust our alarm clock or our mobile phone to help us wake up at the right time.

We trust the work of the laundryman and carry the freshly laundered suit without checking the buttons or zip, even if it is for an important meeting out of town.

We trust the geyser to give us warm water for an enjoyable bath after we run it for 20 minutes.

We trust that our car will take us to our work place.

We trust our digital accessories like BlackBerries and laptops for their memory supports.

We trust the report given by our assistants for the presentation we want to make at a conference.

We trust that the flight or train we take will reach us on time to the venue of our meeting with an important client.

Every morning and evening we trust the local trains and the traffic in our city.

We trust the dabbawalas to deliver our lunch on time.

We trust the NGOs to whom we make donations.

We trust our bank for timely operations and transfer of money to our old parents a thousand miles away.

We trust our laptops, ATMs, pacemakers and a hundred other machines and appliances.

We trust the petrol meter which shows 'Reserve' and comfortably drive till the next petrol pump about 30 km ahead.

We trust the roadside hawker and enjoy his bhel-puri, not worrying about the potential health hazards.

The list could go on and on...

Who says we humans are not trustworthy?

Jumping to Conclusions

It is not given to people to judge what is right or wrong. People have eternally been mistaken and will be mistaken, in nothing more than in what they consider right and wrong.

—LEO TOLSTOY

In May 2004, I had a great time travelling in Kashmir with my friends and family. But the incident I best remember from that vacation has nothing to do with the natural beauty of the valley.

At one point during the trip, walking by the mountains, my son slipped and fell into a muddy pond. His jacket, now dirty, needed a wash. There was a tiny hamlet just ahead, of not more than 15 houses. At a small waterfall, we saw a young girl who looked very badly off. We asked her name and she told us she was called Sana. My wife asked her if she could wash our son's jacket and dry it in the sun and we would collect it and pay her when we returned in a few hours from Chandanwadi, a place that had snow to enjoy. Sana agreed and we went ahead with our plans.

When we returned from Chandanwadi and stopped our car to locate the girl, we could not see anyone around.

We tried calling but no one answered. We got anxious and my son started crying, believing that his jacket was gone. We shared the feeling and murmured about being foolish to trust the girl with the jacket. Why would someone return a costly jacket? We blamed the attitude of the poor and accused them of stealing easily. We even told our taxi driver, who belonged to the same area, what we thought of his people.

We started back for our hotel. About two kilometres later, our driver suddenly stopped the car. He had seen someone running after us in the rear-view mirror.

In a couple of minutes Sana reached us, panting, drenched in sweat, hardly able to speak. Somehow she managed to say, 'Biwiji, aapka coat!' (Madame, your jacket!)

Then she explained that because the jacket was thick and the sun had gone down, she had taken it to the hilltop to dry it. She had sat there for three hours, guarding the jacket from the goats and sheep grazing around.

We were extremely ashamed of ourselves, for all our insensitive thoughts and the comments that we had made a few minutes ago. We thanked Sana and offered her some biscuits and water.

The driver, a proud man now, smiled, as we got back into the taxi. Everyone, including my son, had learnt an important lesson: Delay your judgements, especially about people.

Use People More!

Produce great men, the rest follows.

—WALT WHITMAN

The other day I was talking about a training programme for the retail staff of a supermarket. It was managed by a friend of mine, Nitin Redasani. In the course of our conversation, Nitin made an interesting observation. He said, 'Satish, I love this phrase: People are not useless, they are used less!'

The words are a true depiction of the unused potential of people. Forget the semantics, we are not talking about 'using' in the sense of using someone and then forgetting about them. We are talking about believing that each one of us can deliver, that every person in an organization has the unmatched capacity of leading and doing his or her best, thereby taking himself or herself and the organization to a higher level.

How many times do you let your colleagues make mistakes in their work?

I firmly believe that people will make mistakes only if they work. And if you question them on the mistakes, reprimand them, strike their morale down, you are probably killing their enterprising character. They will then, for fear of failing, never again dare to do the undone or visit the unknown. How would creative growth happen then?

When you see someone make a mistake, do you end up taking the work in your hands, trying to amend the wrong, or do you empower the person with the relevant knowledge and skill so that the mistake is not repeated in future?

Most people in charge of something would, in a similar situation, simply 'take charge' and display triumphant completion. In fact, there is no triumph here. This manager or supervisor has just killed the will in one of his staff to perform, and has created just a follower who will not use his heart and mind in the future.

You cannot supervise subordinates and say that they have not delivered because their efforts, their acts, were wrong. You, as the supervisor, are responsible for the final output. The wrong is in you because the process and method is yours.

If those whom you manage or supervise must grow, you have to give them the wings of empowerment.

You have to believe in people to 'use' them more. This is the only way of making leaders out of people.

A Mother's Age

Attending a programme on 'Regression and Past Lives' by Dr Newton Condavetti, I had the opportunity to listen to some illuminating insights and experiences that some of the participants shared with each other.

One of the participants made a simple but very profound statement about her relationship with her 10-year-old daughter. Whenever she made a mistake in interacting with or understanding her daughter, the lady would apologize to her child and add, 'I hope you understand that I've made a mistake. I, too, am only a 10-year-old mother.' This made both of them comfortable with each other and added a completely new and special dimension to the mother–daughter relationship.

As parents, aren't we as old as our first child? In fact, each child being entirely unique, we are, frankly, only as old as each of our children.

Which gives a whole new meaning to the expression 'Different folks, different strokes'.

Once we accept this fact, we can completely surrender our 'seniority' and the hangover of being more 'experienced'. This transforms us not only as parents but as teachers, managers, leaders, colleagues, spouses, friends...as social beings.

Sanskar

*A child's life is like a piece of paper on which
every passerby leaves a mark.*

—CHINESE PROVERB

*The easy way to teach children the value of
money is to borrow from them.*

—ANONYMOUS

In my city, the HDFC Chowk, or the DSP Bungalow Square as we called it earlier, has been renamed as the 'Kavya Ratnavali Chowk' when the former President of India, Hon. Pratibha-tai Patil, visited the city.

Thanks to her visit, our city got a place, this square, where people come to spend time in the evenings, chatting or lazing around with their families and friends. It is also a regular and favourite spot for my wife and me. We meet our friends here, talk and share a few laughs.

The other day, we managed to find a vacant bench near a flower bed and sat down to chat with our friends, Ratnesh and Smita. Sitting next to us was a couple with their three children, one son and two daughters aged about 10, seven and four.

A dog by the roadside was resting peacefully. The young boy had a piece of bread to feed this dog. He threw it at the dog as if hurling a boomerang. It looked harsh. Serving someone, even if it is only a dog, with this sort of body language, is very rude. The little boy was also pulling his sisters by their legs and hair.

I have a dog at home. Even if by an act of error or oversight, I throw biscuit at him, my nine-year-old daughter Siddhi comes and scolds me, picks up the biscuit pieces and serves him with respect and affection. This probably calls for some reflection on parental behaviour back home. No wonder that couple sitting next to us displayed a strange and tense interaction. They hardly spoke to each other. And at times, when the husband did, he was practically growling at his wife, who took his hostility and insulting remarks without any expression.

Their son was displaying the same aggressive behaviour in his act of feeding the dog insultingly and bullying his younger sisters.

Parents need to check their personal interactions consciously. Else they are creating problems for their own future. They will later complain that their children are rude and disrespectful. It will be a simple case of their own deeds boomeranging on them.

Children love to imitate their parents, who are their role models.

Never forget that you are your child's mirror.

Life's Companion

What greater thing is there for two human souls, than to feel that they are joined for life—to strengthen each other in all labour, to rest on each other in all sorrow, to minister to each other in all pain, to be one with each other in silent unspeakable memories at the moment of the last parting?

—GEORGE ELIOT

It was 23 November 1991, the day I got engaged to my would-be wife, Mitu. Everyone told me that the courtship period would be one of the best of periods of my life, and I would never forget it.

I was wondering why I was getting married in the first place.

I spoke to my friends, my seniors and relatives. The answers were different, and all of them unsatisfactory. They went somewhat like this:

- Progeny
- Societal norms
- Physical needs
- Because everybody does so
- All of the above!

I was not convinced, though I was happy exploring new ways to add joy to my relationship with my would-be spouse. It was too early for me to understand what soulmates were all about.

Then one day, while travelling from one city to another on work, I got talking to a co-passenger. He was about 45. In the course of our conversation, I asked him the question that was on the top of my mind: 'Why do we marry?'

The answer he gave me was, by far, the most convincing one I had ever received. He said, 'It is the premium that you pay for getting insured after the age of 50.'

Each bit of giving that either of us contributes to the relationship in a marriage is helping to strengthen our bonds. The late-night arguments, the after-dinner drive for a paan, the window shopping in malls, the first-day movie shows, watching the train pass by together from a distance, the early morning rising for guests in the house, her sadness during our first few years of marriage when I was only a weekend husband, my travelling for hours by bus to reach her—all of this has nourished the relationship. The heavenly knot is made of all these things, and many more that we do, knowingly or unknowingly.

To tell the truth, I've enjoyed paying the premium for the past 21 years. And today, in my late 40s, I can say, 'In nurturing this divine relationship, you do not even feel the need of ROI (Return on Investment).'

Thanks, Mitu.

Rise in Love!

There is no remedy for love, but to love more.

—HENRY DAVID THOREAU

How can anyone 'fall in love'?

Isn't love something in which you rise up to a higher self of compassion and empathy?

There are so many people who, in a relationship, are hooked only to material or short-lived gains. This could be the first stage. Eventually, however, you must convert those short-term gains to something lasting; the relationship must become a committed exploration of the highest joy of giving.

If it does not, you will build your relations on a fragile foundation. You will indeed 'fall' and never 'rise' in love.

Love is that pure feeling in which one rises higher and higher.

Very often we mistake infatuation or lust for love. Here, again, 'rising' to a higher level will not happen.

How can you help yourself and others rise in love?

You can when you understand that love is all about giving, without expecting returns.

You will have to give your time and actually learn to communicate.

You will have to give your ear and listen.

You will have to give your heart and feel ecstasy.

You will have to give your ego and invite communion.
You will have to give your head and invite sensitivity.
You will have to give up your tears and seek laughter.
You will have to give up your joys and embrace sorrow.
You will have to give up your sorrows and enrich the joys...

And the magical thing is that when you give without expecting, you get much more in return.

Try it. You will only rise higher in love!

Epilogue

Life is really simple, but men insist on making it complicated.

—CONFUCIUS

You don't have to be a venerable old person to discover some great truths about life. If you are observant and responsive to your inner life and all the life unfolding around you, wisdom will come to you.

I received this SMS from my nephew, Nakul, who is ready to graduate as an MBA in biotechnology. He is an extremely lively and energetic young man, and I learn a lot about his generation from his talks and the videos that he shares with me.

The SMS Nakul shared with me went like this:

I was dying to finish high school and start college.
Then I was dying to finish college and start working.
Then I was dying to marry and have children.
Then I was dying for my children to grow old enough so that I could go back to work.
But then I was dying to retire and now—
I'm dying.
And I suddenly realized that I had forgotten to live!
So live every moment of life KING SIZE.
Ye mat socho zindagi mein kitne pal hain,

Ye socho ki ek pal mein kitni zindagi hai!
(Don't think of how many moments life has to offer,
Think how much of life each moment has to offer!)

Acknowledgements

Over the years, as I have evolved as a person and then a success coach (in that order), I have been sustained and guided by several people who are integral to my life and thinking. I must acknowledge them all with extreme gratitude.

My gurus in this journey have been Dr Bharath Chandra of Bengaluru, a behavioral therapist and success coach of international repute; Dr Anand Nadkarni, a renowned psychiatrist of Mumbai; Dr Shubha Thatte, a senior clinical psychologist who taught me REBT (Rational Emotive Behaviour Therapy); and Swami Sukhbodhanandji, who was central to my spiritual evolution. I have also benefited hugely from the timeless work of thinkers and writers like Robin Sharma, Dr Steven Covey, Kenneth Blanchard and Sumanthra Ghoshal.

I thank my friends, Ratnesh Palod, Deepak Sanghavi, and my co-trainer Tushar Chothani for their timely support and a frank feedback, and my nephew, Nakul Mundada, for helping formulate some ideas.

Sagar, Hiren, Dr Tushar, Joshiji and Tushar Phalak—my badminton group—contributed in an indirect but very important manner—they ensured my days began well, kept me upbeat and helped me feel energetic and think clearly through the rest of the day.

Girish Joshi, my college theatre director and writer, read the manuscript and added his professional thoughts as an engaged and intelligent reader. Vandana Atre, a translator whom I met on a train journey, helped with new ideas, and my old friend, and a wonderful writer himself, Harsh Kabra offered valuable advice.

My office staff, Sudhir, Suresh and Rahul for their help and support.

I'm also thankful to the innumerable participants of my programmes and workshops whose questions and feedback were crucial to the evolution of my thinking.

On the home front, I'm grateful to my mother, Yashoda, for her insurmountable will to live and fight against all odds, my brother, Kishor, for his deep understanding of 'kartavya' or duty, my sister-in-law, Varshali, for her strength to be able to smile through everything, my wife, Mitu—who, fortunately, happens to be my best friend as well—for her very justified and always astute comments. Mitu, and my friend Ratnesh Palod and my former relationship manager Girish Pal were, in fact, the first to read my early notes and jottings, and their encouragement gave me the confidence to carry on.

And how can I forget the contribution of my children? My son, Pruthav, and daughter, Siddhi, take away all my stress simply with a smile or yet another question!

Many thanks to Ravi Singh and Dibakar Ghosh for their support. And finally to Rupa Publications for their belief in me.